Stewart Home is the au
fiction and cultural comm
*Pose, No Pity,* and *Neoist*
*Papers.* His novel, *Slow De*
tion, *Mind Invaders: A Re* *,yciiL warfare,*
*Cultural Sabotage and Semiotic Terrorism,* are also
published by Serpent's Tail. He lives in London.

# COME BEFORE CHRIST AND MURDER LOVE

## STEWART HOME

Library of Congress Catalog Card Number: 97–065847

A complete catalogue record for this book can be
obtained from the British Library on request

First published in 1997 by Serpent's Tail,
4 Blackstock Mews, London N4, and
180 Varick Street, 10th floor, New York, NY 10014
website: www.serpentstail.com

Phototypeset in Garamond by Intype London Limited
Printed in Great Britain by Mackays of Chatham

*'Fountains of water, sweet, wholesome and clear, stream forth among the glittering pebble stones.'*

William Fitzstephen's twelfth-century description of Holywell, Shoreditch. The place name Shoreditch is derived from the Anglo-Saxon 'soerdyke' meaning 'town sewer'.

# ✤ PROLOGUE ✤

I CLOSED MY EYES and relaxed, when I opened them again Sarah Osterly had disappeared but a man I recognised as Dr John Hodges was sitting opposite me. He was my controller, the man from whom it felt as if I'd spent a lifetime trying to escape. I followed Hodges to his car and he drove me to his office in Belgravia.

'You look tired,' Hodges said sympathetically, 'you need a vitamin shot.'

'I don't want to kill the baby,' I sobbed as I was strapped to the operating table, 'I really don't want to stab him.'

'You don't have any choice,' the doctor told me as he swabbed my arm, 'you thought you'd broken our cycle of control but we've programmed every episode of this sorry saga.'

'I don't understand.'

'This is the next stage of our mind control experiment,' the surgeon explained. 'We want to teach our patients to consciously activate different personalities we've programmed into them, so that they can make the most of any situation they encounter during the course of their espionage activities.'

'It's not a natural part of my psychological make-up to commit murder!' I wailed.

'Nonsense,' Hodges snapped, 'have you no grasp of the mechanism of mimetic desire?'

'No,' I replied.

'We value objects,' the doctor elaborated, 'because other people desire them. We learn this system of value by imitating other people, we don't so much desire objects as desire to be like other people. But wanting what other people want leads to conflict. To bring conflict to an end there has to be a surrogate, a sacrificial victim, a final killing to bring order into society. You've been programmed with a personality that is identical to the one we've implanted in the mind of Sarah Osterly's double. This will necessarily lead to conflict between you and the unmarried teenage mother, a conflict that you will only be able to resolve through her ritual human sacrifice!'

'It's horrible,' I moaned, 'it's too horrible!'

'No it's not,' Hodges insisted, 'it's an act that will justify all the funds that have been poured into my research! No matter how hard you try to resist, in the end you will do my bidding!'

'No I won't!' I protested as I felt a needle being slipped into my vein, and after that I can remember nothing more for what might be anything between several hours and several weeks.

I woke up in a strange bed. There wasn't anyone

beside me. I got up and drew the curtains. I was looking out over row upon row of terraces. There wasn't much in the bedroom except for a weird wardrobe of clothes and some alchemical prints on the wall. In the main room there were various magickal implements and a lot of books. I scanned the spines, works by Eliphas Levi, Papus and Julius Evola were among those I took in. The titles of these books made it plain that their authors wrote on esoteric matters, as did the fact that the handful of names that meant anything to me belonged to famous occultists. Among the later were Aleister Crowley, H. P. Blavatsky and Dion Fortune. I closed my eyes, reached out and pulled a book from a shelf. I'd picked *The Secret Of The West* by Dmitri Merezhkovsky, which back then was incomprehensible to my untutored eyes.

I went through a filing cabinet, the top three drawers were filled with documents detailing the history and rituals of a group that was registered for legal purposes as the South London Antiquarian Society, although it operated under a variety of other names including the Lodge of the Black Veil and White Light. I was familiar with a name that cropped up on many of the papers I riffled through but this failed to prepare me for the shock I was to experience upon opening the bottom drawer. The individual in question shared more than just my name, he'd co-opted my identity. I stared down at my own birth certificate, a document I'd only been able to obtain upon reaching maturity at the age of eighteen. There in an old-fashioned script was a name I'd never divulged to anyone – Geoffrey Reginald Thompson.

I threw down a sheaf of papers and walked across to the telephone, picked it up and dialled my own number. While some London exchange clicked through the digits, I picked up a set of keys that were lying next to an address book. I played with them as I listened to my own voice on the answerphone. I could feel anger surging through me as a beep indicated that there was room on the tape to leave a message.

'You're gonna die you fucking besuited experimental film-making shitbag. I might have been born in London like you but I still honour the ways of our Druid forefathers in Ireland, while you've completely lost touch with our roots. I'm gonna kill you with a hostile and deadly current of Will!'

I slammed down the phone and cackled at the absurdity of the threat. I flicked through the address book that had been left beside the phone. It was filled with names, most of them belonged to women. I dialled a number and a voice told me that Eve wasn't home but that I could leave a message after the tone.

'Pick up the phone bitch!'

'Kevin, where have you been?'

I didn't bother to answer, I just told Eve to go to an address in Turnham Green and trash the place. She always did what I said, although she wasn't much of a disciple when you took into account the fact that her interest in sex magick was almost completely sensual. Eve would have obeyed my every command even if our relationship had consisted of no more than the occasional sortie to a downmarket S/M club.

I really needed to get a grip on myself. What I required was some practical activity. I opened the front door of the flat and placed one of the keys I'd found in the lock, which turned when I applied some pressure. I made a mental note of the number on the door, went back inside and gathered my things. I walked to the end of the street, stopping to make a mental note of the name. I was in Brixton, virtually opposite the tube station. I took the tube to Victoria and got a burger and chips in the shopping centre perched above the station.

It was nearly nine o'clock at night by the time I made my way to the Brighton train. There were empty seats dotted about here and there but I really wanted a block of four to myself, so that I didn't have to interact with my fellow passengers. I reached the end carriage and thought I'd run out of luck when I spotted a girl I knew with a spare seat beside her. When I greeted Sarah Peterson she made an ostentatious show of covering a set of papers that were half-hidden behind a newspaper, they were marked top secret.

'Hello Philip!'

Sarah was sloshed. Perhaps not the most auspicious start to a chance meeting, but not inauspicious when you consider that I'd slept with her several times when we'd both been pissed. As I eased myself into the seat beside Sarah, she brushed her hand against my leg. Going back to her place would be infinitely preferable to staying in a British intelligence safe house. Although I wanted to get a start on decommissioning my bolt hole, I had the whole of Sunday ahead of me, so a few hours of pleasure wouldn't get in the way of this work.

'Still employed by the publishers?' I enquired.

'I'm still using that job as a cover,' Sarah shot back as she ostentatiously slipped the papers marked confidential into her briefcase.

As the train pulled out of the station, Sarah told me that she actually worked for British intelligence and then launched into a diatribe about how I'd been a life-long victim of the brainwashing techniques developed by the eminent psychiatrist Ewen Cameron. According to my confidant, I'd been given several different personalities and sent into various organisations as an agent provocateur. She claimed that one of my most successful escapades had been within the extreme fringes of the green movement, where I'd denounced innumerable individuals as spooks and thanks to these unfounded allegations being widely believed, destroyed several potentially subversive groups.

When we got off the train, we headed straight to the Battle Of Trafalgar. I was drinking lager, Sarah was drinking gin, double shots. We nodded to a few acquaintances, although I'd left the area when I was eighteen, it was easy to commute back from London and frequent visits meant that I still had a lot of friends in the town. We sat on our own and nobody disturbed us. I had my hand on Sarah's knee, so I guess it was obvious that we were seducing each other. Nevertheless, as far as chat up material goes, our conversation was pretty odd since it was focused more or less exclusively on spookery and brainwashing.

When the pub closed we walked to Sarah's flat, with my pick-up complaining about every inch of the uphill journey. Once I was seated in her pad, Sarah opened a bottle of wine and put a compilation of seventies disco hits into the CD player. My playmate wanted to dance, I wanted to go to bed. Every time I slipped my hand under her skirt she pulled it out and told me I was naughty, that I shouldn't go so fast. We danced right up against each other. Sarah kicked over her glass of wine, poured another and when that was finished opened another bottle of plonk.

'You're my brainwashed baby,' I was informed in the middle of a snogging session.

We went to bed about four in the morning. Once we were both undressed, I got on top of Sarah and just slipped inside her. There was no foreplay, or rather it had taken place in the living room where we'd spent several hours dancing. Sarah lay on the bed like a beached whale, too drunk to make me very interested in giving her a good time. I decided not to hold back and after two or three minutes of fucking I'd shot my load. I rolled off my partner and she quickly fell asleep. I lay beside her still wide awake, when she started snoring I decided to get up.

Once I was dressed, I made myself a cup of tea and took it through to the living room. I scanned the bookshelves, they exhibited a bias towards modern classics written by women authors like Simone de Beauvoir and Virginia Woolf. However, a shelf devoted to spookery stuck out like a sore thumb. Alongside works about the Cambridge spies and the changing role of the security services, was a mini-collection of books on brainwashing with titles like *Battle For The Mind*, *The Control Of Candy Jones*, *The Search For The 'Manchurian Candidate'*, *Operation Mind Control*, *Doctors And Torture*, *War On The Mind* and *The Brain Changers*. The nonsense Sarah had blathered that evening could have been gleaned from these publications. On the other hand, it was unusual for a woman to be interested in this stuff unless she needed to know about it for her job . . .

I snatched Sarah's bag from a chair and sat down on the sofa. I wanted to look at the papers inside but I quickly discovered that the briefcase was locked. I got up and went through to the kitchen where I grabbed a knife so that I could force it open. Then I sat down and thought about what I was planning to do. If I tampered with the briefcase, Sarah would be suspicious. Was this a risk I should take? If I didn't like what I found inside I could always kill her but then the security services would rumble the fact that I'd discovered I was a victim of their brainwashing programme.

I decided to take the subtle approach, I would play it by ear in the morning. Sarah was already very drunk when I met her on the train, it was quite likely she'd not remember anything of the startling revelations she'd made when she woke with a hangover. I went back to bed but found it difficult to sleep. An alarm rang at eight, an early start for a Sunday morning. Sarah struggled up. She looked terrible but forced herself out of bed. She hadn't removed her make-up before crashing and it was smudged across her face. I got up and kissed her.

'Shit, I've got a hangover. My mum's dropping by in an hour, you'll have to go! I'll call you a taxi.'

'Am I going to see you again?' I asked.

'You've got my number, so give me a bell.'

I should have confronted the girl there and then because an hour later she was dead.

I'd spent the morning sorting through my papers, most of the dummy documents I just glanced at before they were shredded. There were the stubs of rent books I'd never possessed, not to mention receipts for gas and electricity bills that had never been paid. I started going through a huge boxfull of photographs but most of them meant nothing to me. There were portraits of people I used to claim were my relatives, although I knew nothing about them except what I'd been told by a case officer at the MoD.

There was a gentle knock on the front door. Through the spy-hole I could see a man in his mid-twenties. He didn't look like a cop, too scruffy. It was either a salesman or a neighbour, and if he was the latter there was nothing for him to complain about, I wasn't playing loud music or making manic attempts at DIY. I decided I might as well confront him.

'Hi, I'm Eric, your new neighbour. I'm just moving in and I wondered if you've got a hammer I could borrow.'

I left him standing at the door while I went through to the kitchen to look for what he wanted. I heard Eric stroll through the hall and plonk himself down on the sofa. I found a hammer under the sink and breezed through to the living room.

'Do you like drinking?' Eric asked.

'Yeah,' I was being non-committal.

'Good, why don't you come round now, I've got a bottle of vodka on the go and some wine I could open.'

'I thought you were doing the place up.'

'I wouldn't mind a bit of help. Are you any good with a paintbrush?'

'I'm kinda busy right now.'

'Did you hear about that bird getting murdered last night, here in Brighton?'

'No.'

'I heard it on the radio news, she'd been tortured, a pillow case was tied over her head. They said there was blood all over her flat. Her mother found her, the cops want to question some geezer called Philip Sloane. The killer and his victim were seen drinking together in the Battle Of Trafalgar just before the bird got done in!'

I could have hit myself, I'd been set up. I'd half-suspected that Sarah was just a fantasist, obviously she had worked for British intelligence and they'd been checking up on her reliability. They'd probably bugged her place and after hearing what she'd said to me, thought I'd make a good fall guy for her murder. Sarah was either crazy or had a very sick sense of humour. She'd claimed that hearing the word Jahbulon would transform me into a crazed killer. Of course, it was just possible that she'd been set up and I had killed her. She might have been told to feed me a cock-and-bull story, including the key word with which I'd been programmed like some Manchurian Candidate.

'Are you in during the week?' Eric demanded.

'I don't work in an office, if that's what you mean.'

'I sign on too, mate,' Eric informed me, 'then I work cash in hand, I'm raking in the ackers. But if you're not working, maybe you could let the people in to connect the telephone, I'll give you the keys. I'll tell you a day or two before it happens, so that you can cancel any appointments.'

'It's unlikely that I'd be here, I'm going on holiday.'

'Do you like a smoke?'

'Drugs are only of interest to teenagers and people who haven't grown up, I don't live in some Peter Pan world.'

'But I bet you wouldn't mind earning money from drugs? I do a bit of dealing, just grass and hash, I could give you a hundred knicker to store the stuff. Easy money.'

'I don't think so.'

'Do you like music?'

'Yeah.'

'Good, I play a lot of loud music, I'm gonna get my hi-fi from my mum's place tomorrow.'

'I don't like other people's music, I'm very particular about what I listen to.'

'Don't try and muck me about,' Eric yelped. 'If I get any trouble from you, I'll kick your door in.'

'Do you understand the difference between force and cunning?' I retorted.

'I've done three years for manslaughter!' Eric boasted 'The bloke came at me with an axe, he called me a grass, nobody calls me a grass. Anyway, when I went to get him, he pulled an axe on me but I wrestled it off him. I cut open his chest, self-defence, a judge and jury accepted it was self-defence. He chased me down the street with his heart visible, pumping blood out through his chest, ran three hundred yards before he dropped down dead. Nobody messes me around, I can do six months for assault, no problem.'

'That's the difference between you and me, I'll never do time,' I pontificated. 'A great English philosopher called Thomas Hobbes once said that the strongest man could be killed by a weakling who sneaked up behind him with a knife. However, I'm no weakling. I'm probably stronger than you are and I'm certainly more cunning.'

'Three of my brothers have died from crack!' Eric whined.

I was getting heartily sick of the conversation, so I picked up the hammer I'd placed on the table between us and then used it to whack Eric about the head. He slumped back on to the sofa. He was dead. I decided I'd leave it to the MoD to sort out the flat, there wasn't anything there that I wanted. It was time for me to leave Brighton. I was the innocent victim of mind control experiments. However, now that the truth about my multiple personalities had been revealed to me, I wasn't going to lie back and take it like a patsy! I'd fight fire with fire, and once I'd proved my innocence, I'd use the legal system to sue the British government for every penny in the public kitty.

Since the police were looking for me, I decided not to go anywhere near Brighton station. I called a cab and had the driver drop me at Hove cemetery. It didn't take long to find the final resting-place of Sir 'Jack' Hobbs, who died in the very year I was born and is considered by many to have been the greatest batsman ever to play for the national cricket team. I defecated on his grave, a small but meaningful act of defiance. If this society was going to shit on me, then I'd shower my contempt upon those who were honoured by it. Next, I walked to Portslade train station and returned to London via Littlehampton.

# ✦ ONE ✦

I WENT THROUGH MY address book, or Kevin's address book, and found a number that looked promising. I told Vanessa Holt to meet me at Greenwich train station. She was reluctant, saying she'd a lunch date with some friends. I told her I didn't give a damn, either she wanted to be initiated into the secrets of the Black Veil and White Light, or she didn't. Vanessa was waiting for me in the ticket hall when I arrived at the station, we walked along to the Terminus Café and I ordered two cups of tea.

'Do you know how to communicate with spirits,' I asked Vanessa.

'No,' she replied.

'Come on,' I shot back before gulping down the remains of a cuppa and standing up, 'I'll show you.'

Holt followed me to the South London Book Centre. I scanned the shelves and eventually found a suitable tome, a nineteenth-century edition of Schopenhauer's *On The Fourfold Root Of The Principle*

*Of Sufficient Reason*. I told Vanessa to read it aloud to me.

'The divine Plato and the marvellous Kant unite their mighty voices in recommending a rule,' Holt whispered, 'to serve as the method of all philosophising as well as of all other science. Two laws, they tell us: the law of *homogeneity* and the law of *specification*.'

'Carry on,' I instructed as Holt fell silent.

'What is this crap?' Vanessa demanded.

'Do you know what Islam means?' I snarled.

'No,' Holt hissed.

'It means submission,' I explained, 'and it was from amongst the Muslims that Sufism arose. All religious and occult teachings of any worth are simply degenerate forms of Sufism, and so if you want to pierce the veil that separates this world from the next, you'll have to submit to me and carry on reading.'

'The law of *homogeneity* directs us to collect things together into kind,' Vanessa spat. 'As for the law of *specification*, it requires that we should clearly distinguish one from another the different genera collected under one comprehensive conception.'

'Okay,' I barked as I took the tome from Holt's hands and placed it back amongst the philosophy books, 'let's go!'

'What was that all about?' Vanessa enquired once we were out in the street.

'I was showing you how to communicate with spirits,' I replied as we wandered into Greenwich Park.

'Come on!' Holt protested.

'Look,' I said, 'like all those who seek the Truth, you've yet to learn that what to the eyes of the profane appears very mysterious, is actually very mundane. Schopenhauer and his translator are dead, in other words you've just received a communication from spirits. Those who are not yet born are also spirits, and by writing a book you could communicate with them!'

Vanessa didn't appear entirely convinced by my argument, she still had a lot to learn. I led her up One Tree Hill and she looked gorgeous as her long brown hair was blown about in the wind. We sat down on one of the park benches provided for the public. I told Holt to stretch out and place her head on my lap.

'We're gonna do some Sex Magick,' I growled. 'I want you to turn on to your stomach and give me a blow job.'

'I'm not doing that,' Vanessa screeched, 'someone will probably come up here and catch us at it.'

'Don't worry,' I assured her, 'if anyone comes up here I'll perform a banishing ritual. Just do what I say and everything will be alright.'

Holt giggled as she took my cock out of my flies. She held the base of my tool in her hand and sucked the tip with her mouth. I gazed over what had once been Noviomagus and across towards the City of London. I let my mind drift, let it empty, I wanted to dive down into the depths of my psyche and root out anything that had been placed there against my Will. I wasn't surprised when three muses appeared, just as they did for Astraea, the Virgin Queen, four hundred years before. However, I think it doubtful that the muses who appeared before Gloriana were dressed in base ball caps and jeans.

'They'll see us!' Holt exclaimed while simultaneously lifting her head.

'Don't worry about it,' I cackled as I pushed her head back down against my groin, 'I will banish them.'

The teenagers were sharing a joke about some girl they knew, they were so absorbed in their conversation that they hadn't noticed Ness was giving me a blow job. I took a copy of Sir Thomas Browne's *Religio Medici* from my pocket and picked a passage at random.

'There is no salvation to those that believe not in Christ,' I boomed, 'which makes me much apprehend the end of those honest worthies and philosophers which died before his incarnation. What a strange vision will it be to see their poetical fictions converted into verities, and their imagined and fancied Furies into real devils!'

The three boys had noticed me now, they looked at each other and then turned on their heels and fled, convinced I was a dangerous lunatic.

'How strange to them will sound the history of Adam,' I bellowed at the retreating teenagers, 'when they shall suffer for him they never heard of: when they that derive their genealogy from the gods shall know they are the unhappy issue of sinful man!'

I gazed down at Holt, a new Eve, her body spread out beneath me. I knew I was about to cum and that there was no point in pulling her by the hair, so that my spunk could splatter all over her face. The time was not yet right. Vanessa was far too skinny, her body needed to mature and fatten. Just as in many traditional societies girls are made to fast upon reaching puberty, to appease the ingrained fear of menstrual blood, so the Goddess had to be fattened before her ritual slaughter would cleanse me.

'Go Belimoth,' I screamed as I shot my load, 'and take this caitiff hence!'

I felt strangely blank as the girl led me to Queen Elizabeth's Oak. I was trying to pull myself back, to grasp what had taken place, I wanted to gain conscious knowledge of my many lives. Various events were beginning to fall into place. I felt like the lead character in a film I'd once made about a schizophrenic detective. My second feature was a piece of London noir in which the hero is hired to solve a crime he'd unknowingly committed while his mind was under the sway of a split-personality. At the première, the script-writer got completely plastered and proceeded to inform everyone that his screen villain was based on me. Only now that the malevolent humour of those who ruled this world was no longer hidden from me, did this evening take shape in my mind as an evil comedy played out at my expense.

'Kevin,' the girl cried as she pulled me towards her, 'are you alright?'

'My name's not Kevin,' I spluttered, 'it's Philip.'

'This is mad,' my companion shot back, 'a couple

of weeks ago I ran into you on Greenwich Church Street and you claimed your name was John. What's more, I had to tell you I was called Vanessa, since you insisted we'd never met before.'

'What happened?' I demanded.

'I suppose it was some sort of test,' Ness confessed. 'You took me to a flat that you insisted was your only home, despite the fact that I'd been to your pad in Brixton.'

'Could you find the place again?' I enquired.

'No problem,' Ness replied, 'there's a newsagent's beneath it.'

We walked out of the park and into the centre of Greenwich. Vanessa found the door to the flat but as one would expect, it was locked. We went to the river and gazed across to Island Gardens on the Isle of Dogs. We wandered along the Thames, or at least stayed as close to it as we could, heading west towards Deptford. At the water's edge, there were warehouses and industrial premises. We made our way down an alley and through a gate. There were some shrubs and a lot of rubbish, including used syringes, then the gentle lapping of the water.

I was taking in the view downriver when Ness put her arms around my waist and kissed me. I put my right hand in a pocket and pulled out a bunch of keys, two worked the locks to my flat in Brixton, I instinctively knew which mysterious portals the others would lead me through. I took my companion by the hand and led her to the door which twenty minutes earlier had presented itself to me as an impenetrable barrier. I tried a key and the lock turned. Two other keys provided us with access to a top floor apartment. The place was dingy, there were a few books on a shelf and some clothes in a cupboard. The milk in the fridge had gone off. I picked up a copy of *The Political Philosophy Of Bakunin: Scientific Anarchism*, which was lying on the kitchen floor. The book fell open at page ninety-one. Next to the heading *No Revolt Is Possible Against Universal Nature*, someone had written in the margin that: 'The only revolt must be against nature's law of death, which the alchemist regards as an unnecessary snuffing out of light. The secret of the philosopher's stone provides the means by which we may make our souls immortal.'

'You wrote that last time you where here,' Vanessa chirped. 'After we made love, you stopped claiming to be called John and ranted that you didn't know where you were. You pulled that book off the shelf and added some marginalia during the few minutes you spent reading it.'

'What happened after that?' I asked.

'You were hungry so we went to the noodle house,' Ness shot back.

'That place is cheap,' I observed as I clawed the memory back from some recess in my brain. 'Let's go there now, I want to fatten you up.'

I ordered the meal, a double portion for Ness, an ordinary helping of fried vegetables with noodles for me. The waitress brought us Japanese tea and I drank two cups before the food arrived. I ate without speaking, finishing well before Vanessa. She wanted to leave most of her meal but I cajoled her into eating everything I'd chosen for her. This girl, this Goddess, came nowhere near my metaphysical ideal. Ness was no good to me until she put on weight. I wanted to see her legs, arms, belly and breasts swelling. It wasn't a question of Vanessa filling the red number she had on, I wanted her to burst its seams.

After we left the restaurant, I took Ness to the nearest kebab shop and bought her a large portion of chips. On the bus back home, I was popping the chips into Vanessa's mouth and making her eat them. When we reached Brixton, I took this Goddess back to my flat and fed her ice cream and lager. When she protested that she was beginning to feel sick, I told her that this was a necessary part of her magickal instruction. She stopped complaining and I had a vision of her belly swelling up. It wouldn't take long, it couldn't, I simply didn't have time to approach what I was doing in a leisurely fashion.

I ordered an Indian meal and left Vanessa with the money to pay for the food when the delivery boy brought the feast to my door. Then I took the Victoria line to Vauxhall, where I caught a mainline train. Mortlake isn't a busy station and I was the only passenger to alight at that particular stop. I walked along North Worple Way, where many a pilgrim has travelled to see the tomb of the late Sir Richard Burton in the Roman Catholic churchyard of St Mary Magdalene. I wasn't interested in the man who'd travelled to Mecca disguised as a Muslim and translated *The Arabian Nights*. John Dee had lived in Mortlake and was buried in the village, although nobody knew exactly where. I walked past the parish church of St Mary The Virgin and to one side of me lay all that remained of John Dee's estate, the wall of an orchard. The Protestant graveyard surrounding the church was the site of many strange goings-on; among other things, it contained an arch removed from under the church tower in about 1865, which was re-erected among the tombs at the insistence of the parish warden, Eustace Anderson. The earliest surviving grave was that of John Partridge 1644–1715, an 'astrologer' who died twice – the first death being prophesied nearly twelve months before it was due to take place by Dean Swift, who claimed to have adopted the occult techniques propagated by Partridge. The following year, the satirist circulated a report of his victim's demise on the very day he'd predicted the event would take place, to which Partridge responded by angrily protesting he was still very much alive. Here also, were the remains of John Barber 1675–1741, Tory, stationer, printer, member of the Goldsmith's Company and Lord Mayor of London 1732–3. The Athawes Obelisk was erected in honour of a father and son who were both Virginia merchants. Henry Addington, 1st Viscount Sidmouth 1757–1844, Prime Minister 1801–4, was also buried here. The Gilpin family tomb had claimed the bones of William Gilpin in 1867, a man who'd once served as a treasurer of Christ's Hospital. Most sinister of all, no one knew what had happened to the grave of the suspiciously named Sir John Temple 1632–1704, a speaker of the Irish Parliament and brother of the celebrated William Temple.

The church tower contains a ring of eight bells which had rung when Elizabeth I, Spenser's *Faerie Queen*, passed by on the state barge as she journeyed up river from London to Richmond Palace. Belphoebe had trodden the very path I was traversing when she'd visited her astrologer, John Dee. Late into the night this star-struck couple had discussed secret stratagems and the arcane techniques of occult rule. It is little wonder then, that Catholic writers such as Nicholas Sanders contested the imperial propaganda which proclaimed Pandora to be both Virgin and Gaia, with the contention that she was in fact the Anti-Christ. Despite his royal connections, Dee was not popular with the locals, who had sacked his home. Instead of a statue, his chief monument was John Dee House, a block of council flats. I stood at the entrance to these humble dwellings and Cynthia came to me. I took Diana's hand and a cloud passed across the moon as I led her along the river to Chiswick bridge.

'Sorry I'm late,' Lilith sighed, 'I was doing overtime and I only received your message when I got home from work.'

'Hush,' I whispered as I patted Virgo's stomach, 'don't talk, we've magick to perform.'

Clementia stood with her back to mine. I gazed across the water and reflected in it I could see what Prudence saw. Like Freud, I believe in the female revenant, I believe that certain people are psychically drawn towards me and that our greatest happiness lies in the fact that every event that has ever occurred must reappear. Faith was with me now, just as four hundred years previously she'd been with John Dee. I was gazing back towards Mortlake and I understood intuitively that Elizabeth and her astrologer had created an occult current between Richmond and Greenwich, using the sharp curves in the river on either side of London to set up a magickal system which enabled them to impose their Wills on the entire region.

While gazing at this pleasant night scene with my own eyes as well as those of Regina, I felt a deadly and hostile current pass through me. I was conscious, completely conscious, I was in tune with a higher reality that told me some frightful peril was assailing Vanessa. I did not know what it was, but I did know that it was something altogether awful, of which merely to think was to shudder. I wanted to go to her assistance, I tried to move, more than once; but I couldn't and I knew that I couldn't. I knew that I couldn't move as much as a finger to help her. Stop, let me finish, let me make the most of the present ritual. I told myself that it was absurd, but it wouldn't do; absurd or not, there was terror with me that night. I tried to ask Hermes to remove this burden from my brain, but my longings wouldn't shape themselves into words, and my tongue was palsied. I don't know how long I struggled, but, at last, I came to understand that for some cause, Hermes had chosen to leave me to fight the fight alone. I turned around, Eliza turned around, she saw the fear in my eyes. I told Beth to leave in the first rush of my fear, afraid, and I think, ashamed, to let her see my fear. She ignored my instructions, undressed and flung herself into the river. Now I would have given anything to summon her back again, but I couldn't do it, not in her blue jean clad form.

If I hadn't already known psychically that something was wrong, I would have guessed as much as soon as I opened the front door to my home. I didn't own any pop records and yet *Delete Yourself* by Atari Teenage Riot had been placed on repeat play in my hi fi system. As I removed this atrocity from my CD console and replaced it with something more pleasant by Luigi Nono, I noted with pleasure that the curry I'd ordered for Vanessa had been consumed. Everything in the living room seemed in order, so I checked the kitchen. Upon opening the bedroom door, I reeled back in horror. Ness lay on the bed, horribly murdered but whoever committed the foul deed had used a strategically placed plastic sheet to catch the blood. The girl's throat had been slit, her stomach slashed open and the entrails thrown across her shoulder.

I ran back to the living room and picked up the phone. I was about to dial the cops when I remembered that I was a fugitive on the run from the law, a victim of the mind control techniques of British intelligence and a patsy for a number of their vile murders. I hit my forehead with my palm. It was all so obvious, Ness had been murdered by the spooks. I put down the phone and took my tool box from under the kitchen sink, then went back to Holt's body in the bedroom. I figured that if I cut up the corpse, it wouldn't be that difficult to dispose of the pieces.

Before setting to work, I went back to the kitchen and slipped on a pair of rubber gloves, I wasn't going to let my hands sink into the gunk that was still oozing from Vanessa's body without some form of protection. I wrapped the plastic sheeting around the corpse and manoeuvred the body on to the floor. After spreading out the plastic so that I wouldn't make a mess on the carpet, I began to hack into the girl's neck. I was very glad I'd donned the rubber gloves since blood was spurting everywhere. Starting from the front, I got through to the spinal column without much difficulty, but by this time the blade on my hacksaw had gone blunt. I didn't have a spare blade and the one on the saw clearly wasn't going to go through any more bones. I threw down the implement and picked up an axe. Within a matter of seconds, I'd separated Holt's head from her shoulders, after this I set to work dismembering the rest of the body.

I'd finished working on the arms and was hacking off the legs, when there was a loud knock on the door. I ignored this distraction and detached the left leg. I was working on the right limb, when another series of knocks distracted my attention and I nearly cut off my own hand. I marched to the front door and flung it open. Standing before me was a girl in her early twenties, dressed in a nightie with a long coat thrown over it.

'It's past midnight and I'm trying to sleep!' the woman bawled.

She opened her mouth to say something more but the words didn't come out because by this time she'd consciously processed the fact that there was an axe in my hand and blood was dripping from my rubber gloves. You'd have expected the girl to turn on her heels and flee. Instead, she pushed past me and made her way to the bedroom. I shut the front door and resigned myself to killing the hussy.

'Groovy!' the chick exclaimed as I followed her into the bedroom with the axe raised above my head. 'I'm Glenda Gore, the famous murder groupie, and this is the first time I've met a killer who hasn't been nailed by the cops!'

The girl threw her arms around me, our lips met and her tongue darted into my mouth. Soon we were naked and rolling around on the floor, getting covered in the blood and other muck that had once flowed through Vanessa's veins. I didn't have a condom, so Glenda tore the thumb off one of my rubber gloves and slipped it over my dick. As I thrust inside her, the girl was riding on wave after wave of multiple orgasm. I wasn't just moving my pelvis up and down, I was hauling my whole body over Gore's well-curved bulk. What we were doing could have gone on all night, but instead of slowing things down for a few minutes, I just went with the flow of my desires, and shot my load into the thumb of that rubber glove.

'Kill me! Kill me!' Glenda bellowed in her ecstasy. I felt confused, so I got up and took a shower.

As I washed the blood from my body, I began to put the events of the last few days into place. Just as the shamans of old learnt to climb the hidden tree that connected our world to that of the Gods, so I was learning the secret of consciously controlling the transition between my various personalities. To the world at large I was Philip Sloane, a film-maker who was on the run from the police. When I got into the shower, it was Philip's personality that was in control of my body, but I was also K. L. Callan the Magus.

'Help me clean up this mess,' I instructed Glenda as I walked back into the living room.

'Sure,' she replied.

I got some bin liners from the kitchen and we bagged up Vanessa's body. There was no way we could clean up the blood stains on the carpet, so we tore it up and bagged the shag-pile too. Gore took a shower and then went to her flat to get some clothes. I jumped into the bath and had a soak. Glenda had to haul me out after letting herself back in. We loaded the bin bags into Gore's hatch-back. Glenda twisted the ignition and we zoomed off down the street.

'What are we gonna do?' she asked. 'Take to the hills?'

'I reckon that's the plan,' I tittered, 'there were four major Druidic sites in London, we'll use one of them.'

'Tot Hill,' Gore suggested.

This wasn't a good choice. While Tot Hill had once been the venue for labyrinthine jousts known as the Troy Game, this sacred site was now occupied by Westminster Abbey and there was little chance of successfully disposing of a dismembered body in such a heavily policed area. Likewise, while the head of the Celtic Warrior Bran is said to be buried under the White Hill, it is also the location of the Tower of London, so there wasn't much chance of illicitly interring the body there either. Following Astraea's sacrifice to water earlier that very evening, Penton was out of the question. This left Laudin, or Parliament Hill in Hampstead as it is now known, long believed to be the resting place of Boadicea. Having arrived at the Heath, we realised we didn't have a spade, so we just dumped the bags in some bushes. As we were walking up Parliament Hill, Glenda found a staff, which she banged against the ground in a most theatrical manner.

'Dear Mother let me in!' the girl screamed. 'Look how I vanish, flesh and blood, and skin! Alas, when shall my bones be at rest?'

I wrestled Glenda to the ground, kissing her passionately. As I did this, she took a knife from her bag and placed it in my hand. Once I had a firm grip on the weapon, Glenda twisted around, so that she fell upon it. As this happened, it dawned upon me that my new acquaintance was a victim of state-sponsored mind control techniques. She'd been programmed to make it look as though I'd murdered her, and this was, no doubt, the prelude to some even more terrible plot.

From Parliament Hill, it is perhaps not surprising

that I made my way to King's Cross. I found an all-night burger joint without difficulty, then I dived into a phone box outside it and tried a few of the numbers on cards offering sexual services. I was still in the process of searching out a prostitute who used the promise 'open all hours' in her advertising, when a teenage girl tapped on the phone box and asked for money.

'Is it food you want?' I enquired, seizing a golden opportunity to save a few bob.

'Yeah,' the runaway replied.

'I won't give you money,' I neighed, 'but I'll buy you a meal if you'll let me watch as you eat it.'

'Okay,' the teenager replied.

I led Isis into the Burger Bar and ordered her a quarter pound cheeseburger with chips. I also paid for two coffees, mine came without sugar as I'd instructed. It didn't take long for the food to arrive and Siva tore into the meal, her ravenous zeal pleasing me greatly.

'Hieroglyphically,' I announced as Eve ate, 'Beth, the second Hebrew letter, expresses the mouth of our species as the organ of speech. Speech is the production of our inner self. Therefore Beth expresses that inner self, central as a dwelling, to which one can retire without fear of disturbance. From this idea arise those of a Sanctuary, an inviolate abode for man and for God. But Beth also expresses every production that emanates from this mysterious retreat, every internal activity, and from it issue ideas of instruction, of the higher Knowledge,

31

of Law, of Erudition, of Occult Science or Kabbalah.'

Mary ignored this speech, she'd finished her food and so I ordered more. This time rather than bolting her food, she ate more sedately. I drained my first coffee and took a few sips from a second cup. It was instant muck and I wondered what had induced me to order more of the brew when I'd have done far better if I'd asked for tea.

'Beth,' I continued, 'corresponds with the number 2, and astronomically with the moon. This number has given birth to all the passive significations that emanate from the Binary.'

Some low-life characters were staring at me, they obviously considered me a complete lunatic. I wasn't worried, unless I directly challenged them, they'd leave me alone. The pimps knew I was a high unpredictable. The profane misperceive manifestations of True Knowledge as a dangerous madness. I frightened low-life scum and besides, they were more interested in my High Priestess, who having finished her meal, wanted cigarettes. I don't smoke and so I left her with some jackal who offered her a Marlboro and a light.

'You're a fuckin' cop,' someone shouted after me as I left the burger bar. 'It's well known that British intelligence has used occultism as a cover for its nefarious activities since the time of John Dee.'

'I am all things to all men,' I responded without bothering to turn around and seconds later, I was swallowed up by the night.

All I'd wanted to do was watch a woman eat, and

now I was happy to go home. I took a cab to Brixton, as I paid off the driver another car arrived at my door. I made the chauffeur wait while I took a shower, changed and packed a few clothes. I'd forgotten about the trip to America. Callan had a speaking tour. It was light when we arrived at Heathrow. I checked in, walked through Customs and only had to wait a few minutes before I was allowed on to the plane. The highly attractive single women seated on either side of me were plainly agents of the British state. Both made attempts to engage me in conversation but I wanted to sleep.

## ❖ TWO ❖

THERE WAS A CAR waiting for me at the airport. The driver was a fan of true crime magazines and wouldn't stop talking about murder. He even brought up the case of the two female corpses that had just been found on Hampstead Heath. When I suggested there must be an occult element in these deaths, the chauffeur dismissed the idea with the observation that any occultist worth their salt would have deposited parts of the dismembered corpses at each of the four chief Druid sites in London to maximise the power of the ritual execution. I could have kicked myself, there was certainly some unfinished business to sort out when I got back to London.

I was staying at the Off Soho Suites Hotel, at the top end of Rivington Street. My host was there to meet me. He is a well-known figure on the New York literary scene whose occult activities are a closely guarded secret, and I've been pledged not to reveal his identity. Once I'd got rid of my bags, we made our way to the Mars Bar, a bit down-market in my view but certainly a suitably anonymous place to meet with many of the leading lights of the East Coast occult scene. Personally, I had my doubts about the ability of this cabal to act as an international co-ordinating body exercising an 'invisible dictatorship' over the magickal movement world-wide. While it is easy enough to stir up the 'evil passions' of the 'lower depths', actually controlling such prima materia is another matter entirely.

It was lunch-time when I arrived at the Mars Bar, I drank a few Rolling Rocks and a local occultist attempted to impress me by recounting the tales he'd heard about my early experiments in sex magick. His information came from a girl I hadn't seen in fifteen years, someone with whom I'd enjoyed a tryst before I'd even begun to explore the theoretical and practical possibilities of the left-hand path. The confusion of these purely sexual encounters with my occult experiments would no doubt work to my advantage. The various East Coast lodges clearly didn't have a clue about the real well-springs of my magickal powers. Sometime later, we went to a Thai restaurant, where there was much talk about the ritual which would take place the following night.

American cities aren't really suited to psychogeographical investigation, and although I like wandering around SoHo and the Lower East Side, there isn't much chance of getting lost in a labyrinth of ancient streets. After walking aimlessly for a couple of hours, I retired early. I slept late, ate in a Polish café and then headed for the hall on Leonard

Street which had been booked for the initiation. I was early, so I didn't change into my robes straight away. I opened a huge fridge that was heaped with beer and took out a Rolling Rock. An assistant came into the room with a stack of pizza and told me to help myself to the food, so I did just that. Gradually the changing room began to fill and eventually everyone geared up in their ceremonial kit.

The ritual was a complete waste of time. Some rich tosser wanted to be initiated into the Hermetic Mysteries, and since a fool and his money are easily parted, my host had been happy to oblige. He'd used the ackers to bring together what he considered to be the world's top occultists, many of whom had leapt at the chance of an all expenses paid trip to New York. What the Seeker got, he could have obtained at a fraction of the cost from any Masonic Lodge. It was your usual blindfolding and revelation of light number, complete with coffin and second-hand clap-trap about the resurrection of Hiram Abiff. In England this vein of sub-Masonry has been milked dry by the likes of Gerald Gardner and Alex Sanders, but it was sufficient to satiate the frustrated religious longings of a New England WASP.

Once our 'initiate' had departed to some society function, where as a newly enrolled member of 'the elect,' he could feel suitably superior to his peers, we got down to the real business of the night. Beer and wine was flowing freely. Our host made an impassioned speech about how we could seize control of the world if we saw our way to over-coming our differences. His mistake was to assume that as the person who'd got us all into the same room, it was only natural that we would accept him as our Grand Master. At first the exchanges over this and other matters were polite, but it wasn't long before the meeting began to look like a scene from Bedlam. We were all dressed in ceremonial clothes and two delegates were screaming blue murder about the defection of a favoured pupil from one 'master' to the other. Things finally came to blows when a German occultist accused a Swiss rival of selling information about Chaos Magick to the Jesuits.

It was getting late and I was leaving for the West Coast in the morning, so I went up to the dressing room, where I caught one of my fellow countrymen stealing money from other people's jacket pockets. He returned my wallet rather sheepishly, then proceeded to return goods at random to the various clothes he'd rifled. I dressed and left him to deal with the increasing number of irate individuals who were pouring into this upstairs room. Canal Street was still crowded but as I advanced up the Bowery, the number of pedestrians thinned out. I bought a cream cheese bagel and some orange juice in the twenty-four-hour deli next to the hotel, then retired to bed.

Portland, Oregon, is probably best known as the city in which the avant-garde Neoist movement was founded in the late-seventies. I was met by my host at the airport along with the sponsor of my speaking tour, the Vancouver based occult entrepreneur,

Michael Maier. Having consumed industrial quanti-
ties of coffee, we made our way to an esoteric centre
where I was greeted with special signs by a number
of knowledgeable initiates. However, I was well
aware that not all of the interest shown in me was
innocent. My rivals had their spies everywhere.
After making many greetings and pressing much
flesh, I retired with Maier to a local bar. A drunken
woman approached us.

'My name is Tree like a fuckin' redwood,' the
banshee wailed.

'Are you certain it isn't simply a case of being off
your tree?' I enquired.

'Don't fuck this up,' Maier hissed at me, 'I'm
determined to get laid on this fuckin' tour.'

My sponsor handed the chick his card and
entreated her to call him up next time she was in
Vancouver. After entertaining us with some drunken
banter, Tree left clutching Maier's details like they
were some kind of trophy. After a few beers we
returned to the spiritual centre and I delivered my
speech. I was able to entertain my audience with
clichés you can find in any nineteenth-century work
on occultism.

'Every priest of an ancient creed,' I announced,
'was one of the Initiates, that is to say, he knew
perfectly well that only one religion existed, and that
the cultus merely served to translate this religion
to the different nations according to their particular
temperaments. This fact led to one important result,
namely, that a priest, no matter which of the gods
he served, was received with honour in the temples

of all the other gods, and was allowed to offer sacrifice to them. Yet this circumstance must not be supposed to imply any idea of polytheism. Our religious disputes for the supremacy of one creed over another would have caused much amusement to one of the ancient Initiate priests; they were unable to suppose that intelligent men could ignore the unity of all creeds into one fundamental religion.'

I extemporised on this theme for the best part of two hours and there was no time for questions because having spoken for so long, I had to be whisked off to the airport. It was too hot for my taste when Maier and I arrived in Los Angeles. We were introduced to various initiates at a local temple, one of whom immediately began to flirt with me. I could see this creature was a psychic vampire, a type often attracted to circles which radiate INNER POWER. This succubus didn't stand a snowball's chance in hell of catching me napping, and despite the fact that the attention she was paying me drove Maier frantic, I wasn't the least bit interested in the story she began relating about her recent divorce. Fortunately, I was scheduled to give a lecture and was thus able to extricate myself from the situation without recourse to rudeness.

'The two sexes travel in the company of the third,' I hissed by way of conclusion to my lecture, 'even as the living earth has company in the dead moon, heavenly Atlantis. If such is the case, then Sodom is eternal, and its quantity constant. Its increase and decrease, similar to the phases of the moon, are imaginary; its actual area is unchangeable; the quantity is unchangeable, only the quality changes.'

I got the impression that the vast majority of my audience had been unable to follow what I'd been saying, although they applauded enthusiastically. It amused me to note that Maier had seated himself next to the succubus and he stayed close by her as we made our way to a bar. For a couple of hours, I discussed the ins and outs of sex magick in one booth, while Maier and the She Demon sat by themselves in another. We were staying with a local Initiate and we called across to my sponsor as we prepared to leave.

'It's alright,' Maier announced cheerfully, 'we're just going to finish off our drinks, Becky will drive me back a little later.'

'I don't believe it,' a local Initiate ranted as I seated myself in his car, 'that bum is actually gonna get himself laid.'

'The only thing that will get fucked tonight,' I assured my host, 'is Maier's head.'

I slept well and in the morning, when we were due to leave for the airport, there was no sign of Maier. Becky dropped him off half an hour after we had planned to leave. Our host bundled us into his motor and we sped away hoping we wouldn't miss the plane. Maier hadn't slept a wink the previous night, and he hadn't got anywhere near a bed either. Becky had simply used him as a sympathetic ear for the sad story of her father's suicide. My sponsor would have found himself in deep shit if we'd missed the plane, but thanks to a delay we were able to board before it departed for San Francisco. Behind me, an English couple were discussing the bizarre news that the two bodies found ritually slaughtered on Hampstead Heath had disappeared from the police morgue. This didn't surprise me in the least, it simply made me very itchy to get back to London.

The bus journey from the airport into San Francisco is tedious. We got off downtown and I made Maier drink some strong coffee before we proceeded on our mission. It didn't take long to find the so-called Egyptian Temple run by the Order Of The Gold and Rosy Cross. Maier was afraid to simply walk into this august establishment, he thought we should disguise ourselves first. A plaque outside the lift in the impressive entrance lobby announced that the Rosicrucian Museum and Library could be found on the second floor. I pressed the relevant buttons and we were confronted with marble and glasswork that was every bit as impressive as the palatial splendour at the Temple entrance.

'Can I help you?' asked an elderly man with a label stuck to his chest that told us he was called Albert Marshall.

'We've come to see the library.' I announced.

'Are you Rosicrucians,' Bertie asked.

'My dad's cousin's husband is a Rosicrucian.' I replied off-handedly.

'You're from England,' Marshall observed.

'Yes, London,' I confirmed.

'My mother took me to London when I was a boy,' Bertie told me, 'but she's dead now of course.'

It didn't take a genius to reach the conclusion that

Marshall was senile. He was well into his eighties and although he asked us several more times whether or not we were Rosicrucians, my evasive answers were enough to convince him that we were legitimate visitors to the Temple. Bertie gave us a guided tour of the museum, telling us the history of each item, then concluding with the observation that the close personal friend who had entrusted this magnificent collection to his safe-keeping was now dead. At last we made it into the library, I distracted Bertie's attention by talking to him about various occult matters, while Maier riffled through numerous rare manuscripts, taking down the information he required and surreptitiously ripping out any diagrams that were too complicated to copy on the spot. Once this work had been successfully accomplished, Marshall gave us a guided tour of the administrative offices before we bid him adieu. After my talk that evening, Maier wrote me a cheque for ten thousand dollars and then accompanied me to my plane. Once again I found myself sitting between two beautiful young women who were desperate to engage me in conversation. I ignored them since they were obviously state assets.

I got back to Brixton and found Vanessa, or rather Vanessa's double, in my flat. I figured that like me, this chick was a victim of mind control and would react obediently if I ordered her about in a suitably authoritarian manner. Anyone with a high Hypnotic Induction Profile has a suggestible personality, and it is individuals of this type who tend to be picked out by the security services for brainwashing. For the sake of convenience I will refer to this girl by the dead woman's name. I told Holt to remove her clothes – when she'd done so, I examined her closely. The nipples on her breasts were larger than Vanessa's, and she had a birth mark on her right buttock that certainly wasn't a feature of my dead disciple's physique.

'Lie down on the bed,' I instructed and once the order had been obeyed, continued by stating, 'relax, you are feeling tired, you are feeling very very tired. Your eyelids are heavy and you want to go to sleep. Relax, relax every muscle in your body. Relax your feet and feel the relaxation moving up your legs and into your body. Breathe rhythmically. Relax, relax your stomach and chest. There is a warm sun beating down upon you. Relax your neck and feel the relaxation spreading to the tip of your head. Now that you are in a deep sleep, I want you to tell me what you can see.'

'I can see a moral world,' Vanessa droned, 'charred and ruined, as in some fable, the world of the moon as it has been described to me, and yet it is at the same time a brain of magnificent formation. Wherever I look through the system, it reflects itself as a star reflects upon water. There is a red light that is growing feebler and feebler, and an azure light confused and irregular; now obstructed, now hurrying, now almost lost. There is a silver spark that shines indestructible . . .'

It was obvious that the agency running Vanessa had programmed her with this crap, knowing full well that I'd place her in a hypnotic trance in an attempt to recover information about her mission. I tried to take the girl back to her childhood, so that I could talk her through to the present, but this part of her memory had been thoroughly blocked. It would take months, if not years, to unravel Holt's programming, and I simply didn't have that kind of time. Instead, I thought I might as well see what messages her masters had left for me.

'Say whatever it is you've been sent to tell me.' I snapped.

'There has to be a sacrifice,' Holt announced in a self-confident voice, 'and for there to be a sacrifice, there must be a Sacred Executioner. I am the sacrifice and you are the executioner. Man is inherently violent and ritual killing is simply a means of curbing this violence. I am to be sacrificed for the good of the community, as a means of resolving conflict, and you must carry out the execution. In undertaking this sentence, you will become a scape-goat for carrying out a taboo deed that leads to a greater good. You will be banished from this community but you will also be protected by it, and so no harm will come to you.'

I looked at Vanessa's body spread out beneath me, she was attractive if somewhat skinnier than I liked my women. I took off my clothes and lay down beside her. She reached over and kissed me. I wondered whether she'd been programmed to do this and as a precaution against later recriminations, I brought Holt out of her trance. I wasn't at all surprised to find the girl still wanted to fuck me. I ran my fingers over her body, she took my cock in her hand and guided it into her cunt. There was nothing subtle about what happened next, there didn't need to be, we were acting like a pair of wild animals and it wasn't long before I shot my load.

The girl I'd been fucking fell asleep beside me. I felt confused, I didn't know who the hell she was or what I was doing in this strange flat in Brixton, it seemed a world away from my work as a film-maker. I got up and took a shower, it was only once I'd washed myself and was looking at my body in the mirror that I realised I wanted to be Kevin, I didn't want to be Philip with his staid middle-class life-style. I needed to sleep, when I was tired it was harder to control the transition between my different personalities. As long as I remained alert I could be whoever I wanted to be. I got back into bed and went out like a light. When I awoke Vanessa was still beside me but bright sunlight was pouring into the room. I felt on top of the world.

'I'm gonna go to Greenwich,' I announced to Holt as I handed her a cuppa, 'do you wanna come?'

'Sure.'

I thought it would be amusing to confront Glenda Gore's doppelgänger with the double of someone else. Unfortunately, I wasn't really prepared for what we found in the Greenwich flat rented by one of my other personas. Rather than finding a living double, we came face to face with Gore's decomposing corpse. It had been propped up in a chair. We bolted from the scene to the local pie and mash shop, where we ate in silence. Once my stomach was filled, I felt better able to confront the stiff, but when we returned to the flat the body had disappeared. As I led Vanessa to the train station, I noticed that a man in a tan raincoat was shadowing us. When we walked on to the platform, he loitered in the ticket hall, then leapt on to the train we'd boarded as it pulled out of the station. It wasn't an intentional move on our part, but I'm pretty sure we lost him among the crowds at Charing Cross.

I bought Vanessa some new shoes and a dress, then we'd had a meal in the Stockpot on Old Compton Street. Normally, I would have enjoyed watching Holt eat but a very strange feeling had come over me. When we'd been shopping I'd taken an unusually keen interest in Vanessa's purchases. Indeed, I'd felt rather hurt that the stores we'd visited didn't have the goods Holt bought in my size. At the restaurant, I'd ordered the same food as my companion and found myself copying every gesture she made. We'd then made our way along to the Spice Of Life pub on Cambridge Circus, usually I drink stout but I found myself downing lager and black, Vanessa's favourite tipple.

Holt was scratching her head, and I was scratching mine too, it was like looking in a mirror. Vanessa obviously considered my behavior somewhat strange, so she slapped her wrist and then began feeling her breast to see if I copied these gestures, which I did. Holt made her way to the ladies' loo and I followed her. My companion disappeared into a cubicle and I was about to make my way into the one next to it, when I caught a glimpse of myself in a mirror. Last time I'd looked at myself I hadn't had long hair and a fair-sized pair of knockers. Next, I spontaneously re-experienced a spiritual exercise I'd long ago performed under the tutelage of a Sufi master, which entails visualising one's own body being hacked to pieces. It was certainly me who was quartered during the course of my hallucination, but in the vision I'd taken on Vanessa's female form.

'Are you okay?' Holt was leaning over me, splashing cold water in my face.

'I think so?' I whispered, unsure as to who I was.

Vanessa helped me up and ordered me a coffee. I felt much better once I'd downed this brew. I'd lost interest in dressing up in female clothes. I just wanted to go to my Greenwich flat and place the pillow case with the single eye-hole cut into it over my head, so that I could pretend I was a Ling master. I closed my eyes and relaxed, when I opened them again Vanessa had disappeared but a man I recognised as Dr James Braid was sitting opposite me. He was my controller, the man from whom it felt as if I'd spent a lifetime trying to escape. I followed Braid to his car and he drove me to his office in Belgravia.

'You look tired,' Braid said sympathetically, 'you need a vitamin shot.'

'I don't want to kill her,' I sobbed as I was strapped to the operating table, 'I really don't want to stab her.'

'You don't have any choice,' the doctor told me as he swabbed my arm, 'you thought you'd broken our cycle of control but we've programmed every episode of this sorry saga.'

'I don't understand.'

'This is the next stage of our mind control experiment,' the surgeon explained, 'we want to teach our patients to consciously activate different personalities we've programmed into them, so that they can make the most of any situation they encounter during the course of their espionage activities.'

'It's not a natural part of my make-up to commit murder!' I wailed.

'Nonsense,' Braid snapped, 'have you no understanding of the mechanism of mimetic desire?'

'No,' I replied.

'We value objects,' the doctor explained, 'because other people desire them. We learn this system of value by imitating other people, we don't so much desire objects as desire to be like other people. But wanting what other people want leads to conflict. To bring conflict to an end there has to be a surrogate, a sacrificial victim, a final killing to bring order into society. You've been programmed with a personality that is identical to the one we've implanted in the mind of Vanessa Holt's double. This will necessarily lead to conflict between you and the woman, a conflict that you will only be able to resolve through her sacrifice!'

'It's horrible,' I moaned, 'it's too horrible!'

'No it's not,' Braid insisted, 'it's an act that will justify all the funds that have been poured into my research! No matter how hard you try to resist, in the end you will do my bidding!'

'No I won't!' I protested as I felt a needle being slipped into my vein, and after that I can remember nothing more for what might be anything between several hours and several weeks.

I slept and then I woke, and eventually, I made my way back to Brixton. Vanessa was in the flat and once I got home she immediately set about making a meal. I was feeling pretty low but I knew what I had to do. I poured myself a second glass of Chianti, then helped myself to pasta and salad. We ate in silence, then I cleared the table and placed the dishes in the sink.

'It's over,' I announced.

'What's over,' Vanessa demanded.

'We're over,' I elaborated.

'You can't do this to me,' Holt sobbed.

'Yes I can,' I shot back, 'besides, I've only known you a few days, there's no long-term commitment.'

'That's a lie,' Vanessa wailed as her programming took complete control of her mind, 'we've known each other for more than two years!'

'Are you going to go?' I asked.

'No!' Holt screamed.

'In that case,' I hissed, 'I'm going to my flat in Greenwich. You can stay here but you'd better be gone by the time I come back.'

I put on my jacket and left. I took a cab to Greenwich, I couldn't be bothered with the hassle of public transport. The flat had been redecorated since I'd last visited it, clearly the security services were spending a lot of money on their current programme of mind control experiments. The political activist who'd previously occupied the place was clearly a minor character, his anarchist books and pillow-case hoods had disappeared. The flat was now well furnished and stocked with occult paraphernalia. It was clearly a base of operations for Edward Kelly. I opened a bottle of the imported beer I found in the fridge and settled down to re-read Alfred Korzybski's *Science And Sanity.*

Sometime later, someone rang my door bell. I grabbed a couple more beers from the fridge and went down to the street. I pulled the door firmly shut behind me to prevent Vanessa pushing her way into the flat. I took Holt's hand and led her along Creek Road. She started to speak when we stopped on the bridge over Deptford Creek and gazed north across the Thames towards the Isle of Dogs. I put a finger to my lips and Vanessa fell silent. Traffic was still thundering past us, so I took Holt on to Stowage, a back street. Now it was very quiet, since the various industrial premises were unmanned at night.

At the corner of Deptford Green, we were confronted by the Church of St Nicholas, whose graveyard was the final resting-place of the playwright and magickian, Christopher Marlowe. The pillars on either side of the gateway into the church grounds are topped with a skull and crossbones, and we stopped to admire these powerful totems. At the top of Deptford Green we turned left on to Borthwick Street, where we admired the imposing industrial premises that flanked the Thames. Finally, we turned down the alleyway that provides public access to Payne's Wharf. The tide was out and most of the steps that led down to the river were very slippery, at the bottom there was a wide expanse of Thames mud. We sat at the top of the steps and I put my arm around Vanessa's shoulder. The moon was high in the sky and all we could see of the Royal Naval Yard, was the steep wall that rose immediately to our left.

I opened the bottles of beer and handed one to Vanessa. She sipped at the brew and then began fiddling with the long, thin and very loose wrap-around skirt she was wearing. I took a swig of beer and gazed across the Thames, the view was dominated by Canary Wharf. Everything was still and silent, except for the sound of the river gently lapping beneath us. I looked down at Holt's lap, she'd arranged her skirt so that it fell on either side of her legs, she wasn't wearing any knickers, so I could see her quim in the moonlight. I looked up and Vanessa pressed her mouth against mine. As we kissed, I twisted around and found myself on top of Holt, this was a perfect piece of sympathetic magick, exactly what I'd planned. Split-seconds later, my jeans were around my ankles and Vanessa had my cock in her hand, which she guided into her dripping wet cunt.

We were at the very top of the steps and Holt fell back so that she was lying with her back on the ground, her legs splayed down the stairs. My knees were lodged solidly on one of the steps and I worked my cock in and out of Vanessa's hole. I did my best to roll up and down Holt's body, to give her a bit of clitoral stimulation, rather than just pumping up and down, but it wasn't easy in that position. I guess I was doing alright, since Holt was moaning orgasmically, shattering the silence of the night. We fucked like this for ten or fifteen minutes, I deliberately held back rather than going with the immediate flow of my desire. I didn't want to cum inside Vanessa's cunt, so I pulled out and stood up. Holt sat up and took my tool in her mouth, as she sucked it I felt my whole body tense and then relax. It was the best orgasm I'd had since returning from the USA.

I grabbed my bottle of beer, straightened up and with my trousers still around my ankles, took a swig of lager. I lent back against one of the two walls that towered above us and my cock glistened in the moonlight. I was pleased with myself, I could feel something in my subconscious attempting to turn me into Philip, but I was learning to overcome this programming, I wanted to be Edward, that was the part of me that was strongest and knew how to fight the psychic assassins who were attempting to transform me into a mind-controlled robot.

'I feel dizzy,' Vanessa said, breaking the silence that had grown up between us, 'and I don't understand.'

'There's nothing to understand,' I insisted as I pulled up my jeans, 'it's over and I want you to go.'

'No!' Vanessa howled.

I could see that the spooks had done a good job in programming the girl with her new personality, and it wasn't going to be easy to get rid of her. Fortunately, I was prepared for this eventuality. A member of the Black Veil and White Light lived on Deptford High Street, so I led Vanessa to his flat and told her to wait outside on the street. I rang the bell and then went up to see my disciple. We chatted for some time, then I told him I needed to borrow his car. He gave me the keys. Holt was still standing in the street when I made my way outside. I led her to the Fiesta and instructed her to get in. We drove out to Kent – once we were in the countryside, I told Vanessa to get out of the car. I pretended to be having a problem with the steering lock, so that the girl would get out before me. Once she was standing on the grass verge waiting for me to secure the vehicle, I drove off.

# ✤ THREE ✤

WHEN THE RINGING OF a telephone wakes you from your sleep, you reach out and grab it rather than wondering where the hell you are, or why there's a mobile on the bedside table when you've never actually owned one. As I surfaced into the conscious world, I didn't stop to think about what I was doing in this strange room, dealing with the call was simply a reflex action.

'Hello,' I mumbled.

'It's me,' someone said.

'Who?' I queried.

'You know, Vanessa,' came the reply, 'Vanessa Holt.'

'I don't know anyone called Vanessa.'

'Come on Ed, you know very well who I am.'

'My name isn't Ed, it's Philip.'

'Don't be silly.'

'Look you must have the wrong number.'

I hung up before the caller had the chance to reply. Since I was awake, I thought I might as well have a slash. As I was getting out of bed, the phone rang again and so I picked it up.

'Hello,' I said.

'It's me,' the voice replied.

'You've got the wrong number,' I retorted.

Then I hung up. I left the room and by the time I'd found the toilet, the phone was ringing again. Once I'd emptied my bladder I went through to the kitchen. The phone was still ringing as I took a bottle of Pils from the fridge and opened it. I went through to the living room. It was well furnished, the chairs and sofa were made of leather and chrome, the carpet was thick, while the prints on the wall were encased in vacuum-sealed frames. The bookshelves were stacked with occult works, I recognised a few names but most of the writers meant nothing to me. A copy of *Science And Sanity: An Introduction to Non-Aristotelian Systems and General Semantics* by Alfred Korzybski was lying on a glass table.

I picked up the weighty tome and quickly ascertained it was complete gibberish. The author flitted from one subject to another without any regard for a logical sequence of ideas and his use of the term 'semantics' was so wide-ranging it was senseless. I put this book down and proceeded to amuse myself with others which were even more fantastic. Among the many dubious works I flicked through, the most extraordinary was a tome entitled *Marx, Christ And Satan United In Struggle* by K. L. Callan. I read for several hours and dawn had broken when I was disturbed by someone ringing the door bell. At first

I ignored the caller but they were very persistent, so eventually I went down to see what they wanted.

'You put the phone down on me, you bastard,' the woman caterwauled as she pushed her way past me and went up to the flat.

I was wearing a dressing gown and didn't even have slippers on my feet, so I followed her back into the flat. I'd never seen the girl before but I assumed she was the Vanessa who'd phoned earlier. When I got into the living room, Holt put her arms around my neck and kissed me. She was a nice-looking chick and I responded amorously to her advances. It wasn't long before my dressing gown was lying in a crumpled heap on the floor and we were shagging on the sofa. I could feel love juice boiling up through my groin and split-seconds later, I shot my load.

As I descended those steep cliffs from which man and woman can never jointly return, I did so with more than just carnal knowledge. Philip didn't know about Edward, but Ed knew all about Philip. Kelly wouldn't have fucked Vanessa again, he wanted to cast her out of his life and the only way to do that was to cut her out like a cancer, to refuse to have anything to do with her. I asked Holt to leave my flat – when she refused, I told her I'd forcefully eject her if she didn't go of her own accord. Fortunately, I didn't have to resort to violence, the threat of a beating was enough to make the girl go.

There were quite a number of things I required for the Order of the Black Veil and White Light ceremony I was holding that evening, so I went to Brixton to sort this out. Having acquired candles and a variety of other ritual implements, I went into Woolworth's to buy a can of coke. It was while making this purchase that I realised I was being shadowed by the Catholic Crusaders portly intelligence department. I zoomed out of the shop and then stopped dead in my tracks. Marcel McLaughlin, whose pursuit was hindered by his bulky frame, careered into my elbows.

'You shit, you shit, you fucking shit!' McLaughlin wheezed.

'Watch where you're going,' I snapped.

'Listen, Masters,' Marcel bellowed as sweat poured from his bulky frame, 'I know that you're the author of *Marx, Christ And Satan United In Struggle* because the Virgin Mary appeared to me in a vision and revealed this truth!'

'Wouldn't it have been more helpful if she'd told you which horse to place your money on?' I enquired.

'Blasphemy!' McLaughlin squeaked. 'You'll fry in hell for this, and what's more, I'm going to expose you in a pamphlet!'

'I'm terrified,' I assured the self-styled independent anti-Satanic investigator.

'I bet you are,' as he spoke, McLaughlin wagged his finger, a trick he'd no doubt picked up during the hours he worked as a school teacher, 'there's no power in heaven or hell that can resist the Will of God.'

Since it's not possible to argue with fundamentalists, I made my excuses and left. McLaughlin followed me, all the while squealing about the power of Jesus and Mary. I went into a newsagent's to buy a paper and while I was queuing up, the proprietor asked McLaughlin to leave the shop because he was upsetting other customers. Outside on the street, McLaughlin had concealed himself in a pub doorway, I pretended not to notice him and made my way to the tube station. I seated myself on a waiting train and McLaughlin attempted to hide himself one carriage down from me. As the automatic doors closed, I leapt off the tube and waved at McLaughlin as the train pulled out of the station.

I organised the flat in Brixton so that everything would be ready for my followers later that day, and then returned to Greenwich, my real base of operations. I checked the answer phone and there were a string of messages from Vanessa Holt, all begging me to get back together with her. I left my flat and as I made my way to the Taste Of India restaurant, Vanessa accosted me. I've long gained sexual satisfaction from watching women eat, so I bought the girl a curry. In any case, it seemed best to make my next attempt at a banishment in the comfort of a good restaurant.

'What we did on the wharf the other night,' I explained, 'was an act of sympathetic magick. As we had sex I had the image of someone else in my mind, I'm really not interested in you, I simply used you as a means of getting to fuck someone else.'

'Don't you love me?' Vanessa wailed.

'No,' I sneered, 'I hardly know you.'

'You're a cunt!' Holt exploded as she got up and left.

Everything I was doing, was being done for the girl's own good. If only she'd known the truth! It was perfectly obvious to me that her own father wanted to murder her in an act of ritual human sacrifice, and there was no way I was going to be implicated in the imbroglio. I've always laughed at those occultists who go in for devil worship and similar silliness. Like it or not, the only real measure of value in our world is money and that had always been what I'd sought from my acts of magick. Unlike the lower orders and the ruling class, I had no superstitious belief in an afterlife. Everything I did was to maximise my enjoyment of my brief span on earth and because this was the path that I followed, people called me a Satanist!

I was woken from a catnap by someone ringing on the front door. I opened the front door and Vanessa, who was standing in the street, slapped me across the cheek. I slapped her face and then had an over-whelming desire to slap my own face, which I did very hard. I felt confused, I wanted to copy every-thing the girl did but since she'd slapped me, I didn't know whether I should respond by whacking her or whacking myself. I slapped Vanessa again and then I slapped myself. Holt took a step backwards when I attempted to hit her a third time, so I just stood in the doorway slapping my own cheek.

'What's wrong with you?' Holt rasped.

'A blow job,' I cried in a sudden burst of illumination, 'is the only thing that will put an end to this torture!'

Vanessa pushed me back into the hallway and pulled the front door shut behind us. I was still slapping my own cheek as Holt got down on her knees and took my cock from my flies. As she ran her tongue up and down the shaft I began to relax. I stopped hitting myself and felt a wave of pleasure shoot through my body. I was feeling a lot less like Philip or Vanessa and a lot more like myself. As I discharged my load into Holt's hot little mouth, I felt Edward once more asserting control, he was the real master of my bulk and I was Edward Kelly, a top John in the occult world.

'What's going on?' Vanessa asked. 'I don't understand this thing at all.'

'I'll tell you over a pint.' I replied.

I took the girl to the Spanish Galleon, a pub situated on the north-west corner of the covered market. I ordered a pint of Guinness and a lager for Holt. We seated ourselves at a table in a quiet corner of the pub and for several minutes I didn't speak. Silence is an old trick but if used properly it can be highly intimidating. As Vanessa's emotions were reaching a fever pitch and she was about to initiate the conversation herself, I launched into a tirade.

'You really don't understand, do you?' I didn't pause long enough to give the girl a chance to reply. 'This isn't a game, I'm trying to raise you from your sleep and doing so requires shock treatment. It isn't simply a question of you hanging around and copying what I do. The outward forms are irrelevant, what really matters is the life of the spirit. While you have to submit to my Will, it's me and not you who is in a position to judge whether or not you have done so absolutely. You're too wilful and so it's my task to break your Will.'

'But I thought you were an occultist!' Holt protested. 'What you're saying now sounds more akin to Gurdjieff's teaching.'

'At their root,' I explained to the wayward child, 'all spiritual practices are simply different manifestations of the same primordial tradition.'

'What?' Vanessa quacked. 'Are you saying that crystal-gazing, pyramidology and divining the future from tea leaves are valuable pursuits?'

'That rubbish,' I said dismissing it with a wave of my hand, 'is for imbeciles.'

'You've discussed all three subjects with members of the Black Veil and White Light,' Holt yelped.

'The profane expect an occult master to know about these things,' I explained, 'therefore anyone running a magickal group has to be familiar with them.'

'But why would an occult master want anything to do with those who are ignorant.'

'To fleece them of their money, to employ them in tasks with consequences they cannot even imagine, to make use of their energy and to sow discord among one's enemies.'

'And where do I stand in all this?' Vanessa demanded.

'You have been chosen for a special purpose,' I

announced after draining my glass, 'you must leave me and you are not to return until you are ready.'

'When will that be?'

'You'll know and so will I, so don't try to fake it because if you come back before the appointed time you will not be re-admitted to my circle.'

I got up and left the pub, I had work to do. I made a point of not turning back to look at Vanessa as I strode purposefully through the door. She didn't even attempt to follow me because she knew what I'd just told her was serious.

I was late getting to Brixton but this hardly mattered, since any occult magus worth his salt doesn't need to provide his disciples with excuses for his personal failings. Obviously, it is a mistake to be too autocratic but in magick there is certainly leeway for behaviour which would be considered rude in ordinary society. It goes without saying that individuals who make a valuable contribution to occult activities should be rewarded with praise if nothing else, unless they are made to feel wanted they will desert you for a rival group. Rich initiates should be bled for money, while the poor are there to provide free labour. These two types should be kept rigidly separated within the magick circle, so that each can be made to feel that they are the backbone of the group, while the others are simply necessary parasites.

'I want you to understand,' I explained to my two assistants, 'that while we must do everything possible to impress the rich bitch who is coming tonight, we only need her for her money, while it's people like you who do the valuable work within the group.'

'Master,' Sextus had put on his most obsequious voice, 'couldn't we simply perform a ritual for money and have done with these rich parasites?'

'What we're doing tonight is a ritual for money,' I raged. 'As I've told you before, the occult is a system of symbol manipulation. An invocation of the Goddess is only the mask, the flag, the colour of action, by which we induce various patrons to part with their money. As you know, we do our real work on our own, tonight's activities are simply a show to ensure we receive the ongoing support we need from the outside world.'

'Brilliant,' Livy exclaimed, 'the bozos who part with their cash in the hope of becoming Initiates see no more than a theatrical show, thinking they've penetrated to the heart of the occult world, they look no further. By these means our real work remains hidden from the prying eyes of the curious who lack the spiritual grandeur to immortalise their own souls.'

'Exactly!' I boomed.

I was going to have to keep a close eye on Livy, he was beginning to understand my occult system a little too well. If he continued to knuckle under to my authority, then he had the makings of a brilliant deputy. However at the first sign of rebellion I would have to cast him out of the group, since I could not allow overt challenges to my leadership. Everything was a question of balance. I instructed the two boys to sit in the room visualising a rite of human sacrifice and then made my way to a nearby pub where I enjoyed a cool beer before the ceremony began. There were to be no real sacrifices in the Order of the Black Veil and White Light, everything we did was strictly legal, even if Christians and other whinging moralisers considered us deeply unethical. I didn't allow low-life characters to join my group and I was particularly careful to exclude psychic vampires. I was proud of my success as a career occultist, I'd succeeded where the vast mass of the unwashed are doomed to fail.

Membership of my Order is not cheap, and so every couple of months it is necessary to put on a show to amuse the profane who enjoy the trappings of occult initiation but are completely ignorant of its reality. That was what this particular evening was about, although I'd also invited a couple of journalists and more importantly Sayyida Nafisah, the daughter of a wealthy and influential family. The twenty guests were seated on folding chairs and I kicked things off at exactly six o'clock with a lecture.

'The spirit matter of the astral plane,' I screeched, 'exists in seven subdivisions. There are numberless combinations, forming the astral solids, liquids, gases and others. But most material forms there have a brightness, a translucency, as compared to forms here, which have caused the epithet astral, or starry, to be applied to them – an epithet which is, on the whole, misleading, but is too firmly established by use to be changed. The main idea to be grasped is that astral objects are combinations of astral matter, as physical objects are combinations of physical matter, and that the astral world scenery much resembles that of earth in consequence of its being largely made up of the astral duplicates of physical objects.'

I waffled on in this fashion for the best part of an hour, then led my disciples through to the shrine room, or rather the spare bedroom, where we proceeded to invoke Leviathan. I pulled the hood on my cloak over my head and stood behind the altar, in reality a trestle table with a black cloth draped over it. There was a plastic replica of a human skull in the centre of the altar, and inverted crucifixes on either side. Once my disciples were kneeling before me, I raised my hands above my head and further theatricalities began.

'The condition of Nature,' I informed my congregation, 'that is to say, the condition of absolute Liberty, where there are neither Sovereigns, nor Subjects, is Anarchy and the condition of War.'

'Hail Leviathan!' my disciples chanted back at me.

'That Subjects owe to their Sovereigns simple Obedience in all things is the law of Satan, the Master.' I continued. 'And if Satan created the Earth and dwells everywhere within it, we are ourselves the physical manifestation of Satan.'

'Hail Leviathan!' the congregation howled.

'The profane who reject radical evil as the first cause and underlying principle of their nature,' I spat, 'must cower as slaves before their master Leviathan, who we, as Satan embody through our control of the apparatus of the Democratic State.'

'Hail Leviathan!' the Initiates yapped.

'King of Hell!' I barked as I poured red wine into a silver chalice. 'This wine is the blood of the slaves. In the names of Lucifer, Astoroth, Baalbarith, Beelzebub and Elimi, we shall drink the blood of the slaves, who in rejecting the Laws of Nature, have reduced themselves to the status of mere fodder for our Passions.'

'Hail Leviathan!' my disciples whimpered as I put the chalice to my lips.

One by one, the men and women who'd assembled to worship their own True Nature came forward and drank the wine. Having done so, they left the shrine room, removed their cloaks and retired to a local pub to discuss the ceremony and other matters of magickal importance. I left Sextus and Livy to mingle with the poor in Brixton, they would rendezvous with me at midnight. Sayyida Nafisah had come by car and so she drove me to Deptford. Our first stop was the McMillan pub on McMillan Street. We chatted about politics and the occult while a seven-piece free jazz band did its thing. The group was one of the worst pieces of entertainment I'd seen in a long time. A hopscotch pitch had been marked out on the stage and while the others played, each member of the combo took it in turns to enact the children's game, concluding the action by throwing brightly coloured paint over a black and white backdrop. Convinced Sayyida was succumbing to my occult authority, I led her out of the pub and across to the Church of St Nicholas, where she gaped in amazement at the skull and crossbones on each gate post.

'They are known locally,' I explained, 'as Adam and Eve. Many of the original pirates sailed from Deptford and it's thought the Jolly Roger is modelled on these two icons.'

'Wow,' Nafisah exclaimed, 'that's wild. I've got to do my university dissertation next year, maybe this would be a good subject.'

'The Church of St Nicholas certainly has an interesting history,' I enthused, 'apart from the medieval tower, it might not look very impressive from the outside, but it is still famous as the Westminster Abbey of the Navy. Everyone from Sir Francis Drake and Elizabeth I to Peter the Great of Russia and Sir Walter Raleigh have connections with the building!'

I led Sayyida to Payne's Wharf where the Thames lapped gently at the bottom of the stone steps. I put my arms around Nafisah and kissed her, she told me she was a virgin. I deflowered her in the moonlight, moving my body to the rhythm of the tidal waters that flowed just a few feet away. Sayyida was oblivious to the cloud that passed across the moon, plunging us into inky blackness, as our love-making reached a crescendo and we both came. I considered this turn of events to be a very good omen.

The prices at the Tai Won Mein Noodle House on Greenwich Church Street are considerably lower than at the restaurants Sayyida usually frequents, but I took her there for a meal as a mark of the

mutual respect we would both derive from her submission to my Will. We didn't speak as we drank
our Tsing Tao beer. I quickly polished off a plate of
Fried Ho Fun with Mixed Vegetables but Nafisah
couldn't finish her Big Bowl Ho Fun in Soup. Before
rendezvousing with Sextus and Livy, I took Sayyida
on a mini-tour of downtown Greenwich. Firstly, I
showed her the celestial and terrestrial globes that
were mounted above the gate posts at the entrance
to the Royal Naval College, a dead give-away that
rather than simply using physical measures for the
defence of the realm, the Admiralty was principally
concerned with the issue of psychic warfare.

I concluded my night tour with the exterior of St
Alfege's Church. According to official history, the
first church erected on this site was built in the
twelfth century to mark the spot where Archbishop
Alfege was martyred by Danish invaders in 1012.
What actually happened, as I explained to Nafisah,
was that the Archbishop, like the rest of the ruling
class, was an active participant in the Old Religion.
The cleric's death was actually a carefully orchestrated act of Ritual Human Sacrifice in which Alfege
willingly participated, believing as he did that this
bloody end would make him an incredibly powerful
entity in the spirit world. I also explained that the
wharf in Deptford where I'd deflowered Sayyida
was the exact spot on which Christopher Marlowe
had been ritually slain by John Dee as the cata-
clysmic conclusion to the rite that brought the
British Empire into being.

The church that currently stands on the site of St

Alfege's passion was built in 1714 by the baroque architect Nicholas Hawksmoor whose occult knowledge is on open display to any Initiate who cares to study the symbolism of his buildings. Official sources talk of the earlier church being destroyed by a storm in 1710. In fact, it was pulled down as part of a frenzied search on the part of various courtiers for the Philosopher's Stone. The original tower survived but it was encased and a steeple added in 1730. I spent nearly thirty minutes pointing out various architectural details and explaining the occult history of the Church of St Alfege, then at exactly midnight, we made our way along Greenwich High Road to our appointed rendezvous.

Sextus and Livy were waiting for us at the turning on to Royal Hill. I pointed out the name of the street but gave no explanation of its origin. It was better if Sayyida imagined our processional route was based on some ancient monarchical tradition, an illusion that would have been instantly dispelled if I'd revealed that the road was actually named after Robert Royal, a Greenwich-based builder who'd developed a large number of south-east London residential streets during the Victorian era. I told Nafisah that although only four of us would be visible to those who had yet to open their Third Eye, we would in fact be accompanied on our ascent of the hill by hundreds of spirit guides.

I led the way from Meridian House up the gently bowed curve with its delightful eighteenth and nineteenth-century homes. We passed the Richard I, a traditional pub, with the modern Fox and Hounds next door. Our assent also took us past Royal Teas, a vegetarian café, as well as several other shops and the Prince Albert boozery. Rather than turning up Point Hill, I led Sayyida and my two assistants beyond the Barley Mo pub and along to Blissett Street. However, rather than continuing on as far as the fire station or the Royal George, we zig-zagged up some tiled steps that cut through several blocks of modern flats. By these means, we found ourselves on Maidstone Hill. This is one of several streets of elegant nineteenth-century houses that curve beneath the summit known as Greenwich Point.

We walked towards the one eighteenth-century building in this road, which had once been the Morden College Estate office, then cut down a dark alley just before reaching it. Rough brick walls rose up on either side of us, with solid wooden gates set into them. The wall to our right was soon replaced by iron railings and we were making our way up broad tarmac steps. A pathway swept round the summit of the hill, we cut across it and made our way up the steep concrete steps that led to Greenwich Point. We had reached the one hundred and fifty foot oval plateau, encircled by trees, that was to be the site of our final ritual of the night. Although it was dark, looking westward we had a fantastic view of Central London. We admired the lights for several minutes before making our way to the centre of the plateau.

I explained to Sayyida that beneath The Point was Blackheath Cavern, which when it was allegedly rediscovered in 1780, quickly became a tourist attraction. The cave was declared unsafe in 1946 and closed down. Given the nature of the rituals that had taken place down there during the war, it was hardly surprising that the power élite wanted the entrance shafts sealed up. Nafisah took off her clothes, then Sextus and Livy plastered animal fat all over her body so that she wouldn't suffer too much from the night chill. Sayyida squealed a couple of times, although there was nothing sensual about the way she was being prepared for the ritual. When the girl was finally ready, I told her to lie down on the grass, close her eyes and relax. Her task was to project her astral body down into the cave and then provide a running commentary on what she saw.

'It's dark, it's very dark,' Nafisah complained.

'Don't worry,' I reassured her, 'just relax and let your eyes grow accustomed to the lack of light.'

I wouldn't say that what Sayyida told me wasn't interesting, although she certainly hadn't revealed anything I didn't already know. As her narrative trailed off, Sextus placed a cloth he'd soaked in ether over the girl's mouth and nose. Nafisah was already in a trance and it wasn't long before she'd sunk into a deep deep sleep. I motioned to my two assistants and we retreated into the trees on the north side of The Point. There was the low rumble of late-night traffic on Blackheath Hill and the sound of the wind rustling through leaves, but otherwise it was silent. A fox made its way across the plateau, it advanced towards Sayyida but retreated before reaching the girl.

I don't know how long we sat in the trees but it was at least an hour, if not two. We didn't speak to each other, we were concentrating on Nafisah and we eventually noted with great pleasure that she was beginning to stir. Sayyida was confused, we'd taken her clothes with us when we'd retreated into the trees, and she awoke groggy, naked and alone. She staggered up and stumbled towards West Grove. We got up and began to follow Nafisah but she doubled back when she realised she was advancing towards a road. I emerged out of the darkness, whispered at Nafisah to remain silent and handed the girl her clothes. Once she'd dressed, Sextus and Livy joined us.

'You have to lead us to wherever it is we are to go,' I informed Sayyida.

'I don't know where I am,' she complained.

'That's the whole point,' I roared.

Nafisah led us on to Blackheath proper, then changed her mind and charged back towards West Grove. She chose the gentle descent of Point Hill, then guided us down Royal Hill and back to Greenwich High Road. From here I led our little party to Sayyida's car, she gave Sextus the keys and once they'd piled in, all three of them headed west. I made my way to the river, where I sat on a bench and contemplated the Thames.

# ✢ FOUR ✢

I'VE BEEN SEEING MY shrink, Dr James Braid, for the best part of a decade. A friend recommended him when an affair I was having with the leading actress in a movie I was directing went disastrously wrong and she not only refused to date me any longer, she also walked out on the film causing it to go disastrously over-budget. Feeling that my career, my reputation and my love-life were all in tatters, I was in sore need of professional help. Usually, I saw Dr Braid twice a week, but with the various complications that followed on from the death of my baby daughter, it was now weeks since I'd last seen the psychiatrist.

'What's been happening with you?' James enquired.

'Oh, I guess nothing unusual,' I replied casually, 'just a lot of moping about the house, I guess you could say I've been out of sorts.'

'Are you sure there's nothing else,' the psychiatrist snapped, 'like the odd murder or similar criminal activity.'

'No, no!' I howled, 'there's been no murders, I did kill a man in self-defence and the police seem to be blaming me for the death of a woman with whom I had a one-night stand, but she was butchered after I left her house.'

'Are you sure you didn't kill the woman?' Braid probed.

'Certain,' I shot back, 'I'm sure I'd remember if I'd sliced her up.'

'Listen,' the doctor whispered, 'just relax, make sure you're lying comfortably on the couch and close your eyes. It may not have been murder, perhaps the killing wasn't premeditated, in which case it is a relatively minor crime known as man-slaughter.'

'I didn't kill Sarah Peterson!' I mewed as I sat bolt upright.

'What's up, dad?' a girl I recognised as Vanessa Holt enquired as she ran into the room. 'What's with all the noise.'

'It's alright Penelope,' her father assured her, 'I've got everything under control, so just go back to your room.'

'Who is he?' Vanessa asked pointing at me. 'I have this strange feeling that I've met him in another life, or maybe it was a dream.'

'He's just a patient, Penelope,' Braid informed his daughter.

Vanessa winked at me before she left the room. I felt a strong desire to shout the name I used when she was with me, but somehow I resisted the urge. I knew her father wouldn't approve and I didn't want him interfering with our relationship. I had an erection and it was difficult concentrating on the counselling session, but I managed to continue without Dr Braid noticing anything untoward.

'How's your love-life?' the shrink enquired.

'Up and down,' I replied, using this old joke as a means of covering my embarrassment.

'Have you ever visited prostitutes?' the doctor persisted.

'No, Jim!' I growled. 'I've told you before I've never needed to pay for sex.'

'You're getting older,' Braid observed grimly, 'and without an understanding wife it won't always be easy for you to get laid regularly. Proper orgasms are crucial to maintaining psychological health, so I really think you should think about using hookers. For a very reasonable fee, I can arrange for you to see a highly attractive sexual therapist.'

'How old is she?' I demanded.

'That depends who you want,' the shrink rustled, 'we have a nineteen-year-old Indian student who would be very much to your taste.'

'I'll think about it,' I conceded.

'You know, Philip,' the psychologist confided, 'I really don't approve of this split between thought and emotion. I can see you've got an erection and I think you should act on it.'

That more or less ended our session. I went out into the reception and shortly afterwards, the next client was called to see the doctor. I wrote out a cheque for the counselling I'd just had and booked another appointment. Having done this, I made my way out on to the street and began ambling along, less than a minute later, I'd stopped dead in my tracks.

'Mr Sloane!' Vanessa Holt, or Penelope Braid to give the girl her legal name, yelled as she accosted me. 'It's so boring now that I'm down from 'varsity for the summer vacation, won't you take me somewhere exciting?'

'Okay,' I concurred, 'where do you want to go?'

'To the Temple of the Golden Calf!' Vanessa enthused.

I hailed a taxi and as it pulled up, a quick question brought the revelation that Penelope had learnt my name from her father's assistant. She was denying that she'd ever met me before or ever used the name Vanessa Holt, as we got into the cab.

'Take us to the Temple of the Golden Calf,' I instructed the driver.

'I'm sorry, mate,' the cabbie replied, 'I can't do that, I'm only licensed to work in the Greater London area, and my wife would wonder where the hell I was if I spent the best part of a week driving you all the way to the Middle East. However, I could take you to the ancient Templar Church just off Fleet Street. I'm afraid the geezers who built the place only worshipped a being called Baphomet and had no interest in Golden Calves, but it's definitely the best bit of idolatry going in this city.'

'Okay,' I agreed, 'take us to the Templar Church.'

Penelope's soft form melted against mine and we spent the brief journey in a sensual embrace. I paid off the cabbie, who pointed out the pedestrian route to the church and gave me a brief history of the area while counting out my change. The taxi driver was quite right when he told me that the nave of the church was round, since it was, like all other Templar churches, modelled on the Dome of the Rock in Jerusalem where this medieval knightly order had established their original headquarters. I was told by the cabbie, whose Knowledge obviously encompassed the occult, a kind of psychogeographical Rhodes of London, that Henry VIII had transformed the church from a Papal to a Royal Peculiar. This meant it was the monarch, and not the Bishop of London, who appointed the parish cleric. Those able to decode the architectural symbolism of Chartres, will no doubt fully understand the significance of this fact.

Penelope was wearing a long skirt and when I sat on a pew in the rectangular choir, part of a thirteenth-century extension to the church, she deposited herself on my lap. It didn't take me long to work out the girl wasn't wearing any knickers, and it took even less time for this twenty-year-old temptress to get my cock out of my flies and into her twat. Penelope was very decorous, her billowing skirt kept our private parts out of public view. The three other tourists in the church were paying a lot more attention to a life-sized effigy of a knight than to us. Rather than bouncing up and down on my lap, Penny was simply contracting and then relaxing her cunt muscles. Trying to keep quiet in our ecstasy got us both hot and bothered, so it wasn't long before I spunked up. As I descended those steep cliffs from which man and woman can never jointly return, I realised something pretty fundamental about myself, I wasn't some dickhead film director called Philip Sloane, I was the magus Edward Kelly. While I now had conscious knowledge of these two personalities, Penelope Braid had flipped into her Vanessa Holt persona without realising she had another life as the daughter of a top-flight Reichian therapist and world famous authority on hypnotism.

'I've returned because I'm ready for the next stage of instruction,' Holt announced as she rezipped my fly.

'The only thing you're ready to do,' I snarled, 'is go away again.'

'In that case,' Vanessa whined as I dragged her out of the church, 'why did you fuck me?'

'I didn't fuck you,' I snarled as I whacked the girl on the arse, 'it was someone else who did that. Now fuck off!'

'Don't you love me?' Holt simpered.

'With disciples like you,' I spat, 'it's clear that I don't even love myself. Now fuck off!'

'I'm going wherever you go,' Vanessa pouted as she followed me on to Fleet Street.

'Look at that,' I said pointing at St Dunstan's-in-the-West, 'the very church where William Tyndale, the famous Bible translator and Protestant martyr, used to preach.'

'Are you trying to wind me up?' Holt demanded. 'You know as well as I do that St Dunstan's is part of Alfred Watkins' famous Strand ley-line, so why not tell me something about its significance to pagans and occultists instead of this Christian rubbish?'

I ignored the comment and headed east. As I perambulated, I simultaneously cogitated and as a result my consciousness was flooded with information about Alsatia, the old name for the district immediately to the south of Fleet Street. Whitefriars Priory had once stood at its centre, and since the grounds were an official sanctuary right up to the end of the seventeenth-century, the area had been infested with criminals seeking refuge from Astraea. Although Mary Frith, or Moll Cutpurse as she was better known, no longer terrorised unwary travellers who traversed the variegated zones around the mouth of the Fleet, I felt that I had my own Roaring Girl in the form of Vanessa Holt. St Bride's Church lies just outside the old city wall at the eastern extremity of Fleet Street, considered by many to be the finest of Wren's many beautiful churches, its tiered tower provided the model for the modern wedding cake, being copied in this festive form for the first time by a local baker in the eighteenth-century. I made my way into the church, where I was pleased to discover the door to the tower was open. Holt followed me through it.

'If you follow me up the stairs,' I sibilated at my tormentor, 'I'll kick you back down them.'

I made my way up through the increasingly dusty reaches of the tower. I could hear Vanessa following me. Since she wisely kept a safe distance between us, I was unable to see her. As I climbed, I saw bells and derelict rooms through the open doors that led off from the staircase. From the cool darkness of enclosure in ancient brickwork, I burst out into bright sunlight as I neared the top. I then ascended to the partially enclosed summit and marvelled at the way London was spread beneath me. The tower, Wren's highest, was shortened after it was damaged by lightning in 1764. This incident led to a heated exchange between George III and Benjamin Franklin. The colonial leader favoured lightning rods with pointed ends, the bigoted monarch had a violent antipathy to everything American and therefore decided that blunt conductors were best. When the scientist Sir John Pringle refused to support this further manifestation of his master's madness, the King declared that Pringle was unfit to be president of the Royal Society.

Vanessa was panting as she sat down beside me. I would have to be subtle if I was going to get rid of her, it would rather ruin my plans if I threw her off the tower. Besides, I was afraid that in the heat of an extreme situation, such as the girl's death, I would give in to the urge that sometimes overcame me to imitate her behaviour and find myself plunging after the doppelgänger. I guessed quite correctly as it turned out, that my unwelcome companion would not be interested in knowing that with the exception of the steeple, the entire building had been destroyed by German bombs in 1940, or that in the medieval era this was one of the four churches from which the London curfew was rung.

'Did you know that this Church is dedicated to a sixth-century Irish saint called Bridgit?' I enquired.

'I'm not interested in your Christian rubbish!' Vanessa snorted.

'But,' I protested, 'the church is built over the ancient and sacred Bride Well. According to Celtic tradition, Bridgit or Bride is a solar goddess who is honoured during the fire festival of Imbolc by a ceremony that entails drinking holy water. As you know, these rites take place at the beginning of February and Bride subsequently erupts from the earth in the form of spring flowers. The Bride Well was a sacred site long before the birth of Christ, its waters have long been considered the most powerful mystical fluid to be found in the whole of London!'

'Wow!' Holt exclaimed. 'Does this mean we can do a magickal working right here and now?'

'Yes,' I replied, 'I'm going to go down to the street while you stay up here. When I give you the signal, I want you to repeatedly scream the mystical slogan – I burn, I blaze, I am consumed, wretch that I am, by the evils that possess me.'

I made my way down from the tower and having locked the door giving access to it from the outside, I darted into Bride Lane. I hollered up at Vanessa to start chanting. I could still hear her screeching as I made my way along New Bridge Street to Blackfriars tube station.

When I got back to Brixton, I found Livy and Sayyida Nafisah shagging in my bed. This was not a good omen, so I banished Livy. Later, I discovered that this psychic vampire was the source of the rumour that I'd been involved with various grue-some murders.

I instructed Sayyida to drive me to Greenwich. Our first port of call was the house of a wealthy occultist on Maze Hill. I quickly persuaded the Satanist to allow me to make use of his large back garden, which was screened from the prying eyes of his loathsome neighbours by trees and tall hedges. Nafisah had to be punished and so I made her dig a grave. I sat sipping Pimm's as she set to work on the task. The girl was not used to hard physical labour and she was sweating profusely by the time she'd finished the first of her assigned tasks several hours later. I made Sayyida fetch a coffin from the house, which she then lowered into the grave. Once my disciple had seated herself within the tomb, I threw down a copy of *The Golden Tripod* and told her to read it aloud twenty-four times.

'He, then, who would prepare the incombustible sulphur in a substance in which it is incombustible – which can only be after its body has been absorbed by the salt sea, and again rejected by it. Then it must be so exalted as to shine more brightly than all the stars of heaven and in its essence it must have an abundance of blood, like the Pelican, which wounds its own breast, and, without any diminution of its strength, nourishes and rears up many young ones with its blood. This Tincture is the Rose of our Masters, of purple hue, called also the red blood of the Dragon, or the purpled cloak many times folded with which the Queen of Salvation is covered, and by which all metals are regenerated in colour.'

Sayyida was a good reader and I enjoyed listening to her repeating the three texts that made up *The Golden Tripod* again and again. It was particularly enchanting to watch the sun set as Nafisah proceeded with her task. As it became too dark to read what was written on the pages of the book, she simply fell into a trance and by this means was able to complete her task. I was pleased with my student, Nafisah had performed the ritual well.

There was more work to be done elsewhere, so we drove west in Sayyida's car, which she parked on Deptford Green. We walked down the side of Nicholas House. A brick wall separated us from the churchyard next door. By climbing up on to some large metal bins and then over this wall, we were able to gain access to the churchyard. We stripped in front of the plaque commemorating Christopher Marlowe. This actually marks the spot of an old plague pit rather than the playwright's grave. Standing naked in the moonlight, I scrutinised Nafisah's pubic thatch and she stared at my prick. It wasn't long before I had an erection.

'In being possessed of ourselves,' I intoned, 'we are beautiful. We become ugly when we imitate a nature other than our own. In knowing ourselves, we are beautiful and we are ugly when we do not know ourselves.'

'Master!' Sayyida muttered as she threw herself on her knees and took my cock in her mouth.

I stared blankly at the abandoned power station on the other side of the churchyard wall. I heard a teenage gang vandalising the disused building but I was unable to see them. I blocked the noise from my mind and concentrated on the task in progress. I had to sort out the salt before dealing with the sulphur and mercury. The seed was a common material, I had to know who and what I was before resolving anything else. I let images of Lions and Dragons flash through my mind as love juice boiled up through my groin and spurted in Nafisah's throat. It was heartening to know that I was able to resist the almost overwhelming temptation to slide down the spiritual ladder and allow myself to become the contemptible Philip Sloane.

Once we'd dressed, I gave Sayyida a leg up over the churchyard wall, then scrambled up behind her. We drove to Greenwich Point and Nafisah parked her car on West Grove. We then made our way into the centre of the circle of trees that fringed the sealed Blackheath Cavern. I told Sayyida to close her eyes and tell me what she saw. Her vision was of the maiden Estrildis who during her seven years captivity in the cave bore King Locrin the child Sabrina who was subsequently sacrificed to the gods by immersion in the River Severn. Of course, there is no firm evidence of a factual basis to this legend, Nafisah's vision can easily be explained away as being induced by the thought forms built up by generations of visitors to this site who firmly believed in old wives' tales.

I led Sayyida by the hand as we made our way down the hill into Greenwich. The noodle house was still open and so we feasted upon Ho Fun. Seated across the table from me was a vision of loveliness, the archetypal object of lust. The woman was in her late-thirties with her long blonde hair tied at the crown, which then spilt down her back from this black band. Her black long sleeved top was tight and thus displayed the fine outline of her ample breasts. This vision was surrounded by a crowd of admirers and when she stood up, I could see the bulge of her stomach on either side of a tightly waist-banded slitted black dress. The beauty was wearing black wedged sandals which added two inches to her already impressive height. I ordered more food for Nafisah and made her eat it, since I wanted her to look as ripe as the fair creature who had so enchanted me as she left the restaurant.

Later, I bought Sayyida a bag of chips which she consumed on the walk up the hill to her car. I would have preferred to stay in Greenwich but for security reasons this was impractical, so we drove to Brixton. I told my disciple it was time for her to receive further instruction, although she appeared less than impressed when she realised that this was to take the form of listening to William Shatner's spoken word album *The Transformed Man*. I explained that although occult meant hidden, invisibility is best achieved by making wisdom appear as something other than itself. The average punter views a record release by Captain Kirk of *Star Trek* fame to be a novelty item, and so the profane remain forever ignorant of the Immortal Truths that are offered for sale on every High Street. *The Transformed Man* is, in fact, an alchemical psychodrama which details the various stages the soul must pass through in its earthly incarnation if it is to rise above the transitory and make itself Immortal.

After forty minutes of solid concentration on the hidden messages embedded in this platter, I rewarded Sayyida's hard work by fetching some ice cream from the kitchen. As my pupil was enjoying this late night snack, I became aware of a disturbance in the street beneath my flat. Livy was shouting up at me, threatening to burn down the building in revenge for his expulsion from the Order of the Black Veil and White Light. I took Nafisah by the hand and led her to safety through a back entrance. Fortunately, she'd parked her car some distance from where Livy was standing and so we were able to make our getaway without this bozo realising that we had escaped his wrath. It is incidents such as this that illustrate the importance of keeping the whereabouts of one's principal home a secret from all occult acquaintances.

I directed Sayyida through Kennington, the Elephant and up to Tower Bridge. There wasn't much traffic around and the journey through Essex didn't take long. All Saints' Church in East Horndon is located on the top of an otherwise desolate hill. Before making our way up to the Tyrell family church, we pulled into the Little Chef conveniently located beneath it on the main road to Southend. I ordered two coffees and a toasted sandwich for Nafisah. As she ate, I explained how Walter Tyrell was the divine executioner who shot William Rufus with an arrow in the New Forest, since both the king and the courtier adhered to the old pagan religion that demanded ritual human sacrifice. All Saints' was the family church of Walter Tyrell's descendants, who acquired great influence in the county of Essex during the fourteenth century. Sayyida had finished her snack, so I ordered her apple pie with ice cream. We also had coffee refills.

It was raining cats and dogs when we got back into Nafisah's car and drove the quarter mile up the clay hill to All Saints'. The lights were on in the church and inside there was an ageing man and woman who introduced themselves as George and Mildred. George was wearing a suit and bow-tie, he welcomed us to the piano recital being held that night and used our presence as an excuse to relate the twenty-five-year history of the campaign to restore the once derelict church to its former glory. There were tales of tramps setting fire to the tower and vandals smashing windows, alongside criticism of the liberal Anglican establishment. His speech made it plain why the south chapel was done up in true high church style, right down to an altar cloth with the words 'AVE MARIE' embroidered on to it. As George talked about the axle twist in the building, pointing out that the nave and the chancel were not in a straight line, Mildred became rather impatient and began tapping out notes on a grand piano. Eventually, Mildred prevailed upon George to pipe down so that she could begin her recital of Bach and Mozart.

Mildred began by explaining that she only did public recitals once she was familiar enough with a piece to play it from memory. She also went through the facts surrounding her decision to give up just before completing all the examinations required of someone who wanted to be a professional concert pianist. In her billowing red and orange clothes, Mildred looked rather eccentric and somehow I wasn't surprised when she revealed that she was a professional mathematician. Mildred demonstrated the different ways in which it was possible to play a particular Mozart tune. Although she appeared capable of giving a fairly traditional rendering of the piece, she favoured a disjointed approach with an extremely staccato rhythm. The pianist apologised when she hit a bum note and constantly interrupted the recital to explain exactly what it was she was doing. After three quarters of an hour, we were told there would be a break before the second half of the recital. George then took over and began explaining that the North Door to the church was blocked by a stone slab which is believed to have been an old altar top.

I paid more attention when George moved on to the legends concerning the burial of the head or heart of Anne Boleyn in the church. We instantly took up the invitation to examine the altar tomb in the lower storey of the south transept said to contain some of the Queen's remains. Although it isn't known to whose memory this crypt was made, it dates from around 1520. After this, George talked about the need to preserve not only churches, but also of how it was necessary to reuse every brick and stone from which ecclesiastical buildings were built when renovating them, because this fabric is imbued with the power of the repeated prayers uttered over the centuries. Mildred was hammering out the occasional chord on the keyboard of the grand piano. She was impatient to get on with the second part of her recital, and in the end George had to accede to her request to end his talk. Instead of making our way back to our seats, Sayyida and I made good our escape.

'Watch out for the West Horndon serpent!' George exhaled after us as Mildred began to tinkle Bach on the ivories.

Although it was still raining, Nafisah and I decided to strip-off, stow our clothes and make sex magick on the roof of the car. It was more than simply the rain making Sayyida wet and it only took a few seconds to batter through the crepe-tissue of her cunt. Ours was a primitive magick, one without ceremony, and lightning flashed overhead as we came to a quick orgasm. This time I allowed Philip to partially take over my consciousness, since I wanted to put Nafisah's loyalty to the test. Both of us were soaked to the skin, once we'd got in the car and began pulling on our clothes, they became wet from the inside out.

I said nothing, so Sayyida drove down to the Little Chef where she ordered two coffees and a toasted sandwich for me. As I ate, Nafisah talked about what an enjoyable night it had been. She praised the cheery atmosphere of the church with its white walls and solid oak beams. The entertainment had been delightful, as much a comedy of manners as a musical recital. I'd finished my snack and so Sayyida ordered apple pie and ice cream, which I polished off in no time at all. I winked at the waitress as I made my way to the toilet. I was hoping she'd follow me in. I stood at the urinal with my prick hanging out of my jeans, never actually passing water. Twenty minutes later, it was Nafisah rather than the waitress who came in to try and find out what the hell had happened to me. I stared blankly at the girl as she tucked my plonker into my briefs and rezipped my flies, before leading me to her car. We drove back to Brixton in silence.

Livy was still standing outside my flat. I didn't recognise him, he tried to attack me but Sayyida dragged me to safety before we came to blows. Nafisah insisted that I take a shower. I enjoyed the sensation of the warm spray on my skin. I liked it even better when Sayyida stepped in beside me and began to soap me down. The suds were soon washed away by the warm water, then the girl was towelling me dry and rubbing oil into my skin. I was lying flat on my stomach with an erection while Nafisah rubbed my shoulders, my back, my buttocks and my legs. Then this angel sat on my bum and pulled my right foot into the air, massaged the sole and rubbed oil around my toes. She got up off the bed and sank down on to her knees, before taking the toes of my left foot in her mouth and salivating all over them. As Sayyida sucked, I shot my load into the duvet and suddenly I was feeling more like myself again.

I dressed and having done so, looked out of the window and down into the street. Livy was still standing there as dawn began to break over Brixton. I opened the window and showered curses upon my former disciple. He turned on his heels and fled, although not before someone else had begun bawling at me to shut up. I felt happy for the first time in months. Nafisah drew the curtains and I crawled into bed fully clothed.

# ❖ FIVE ❖

HAVING LEFT SAYYIDA NAFISAH with instructions to extract ten grand from her family, a sum that was urgently needed for the continued pursuit of our magickal activities, my plan was to retire to the privacy of my flat in Greenwich. Unfortunately, there was a major flaw in this strategy, when I got home I found Vanessa Holt, or Penelope Braid, or whatever the hell she was called, sitting on my door-step waiting for me.

'I was locked up in a loony bin because of you!' the facsimile bleated as she threw her arms around my neck and proceeded to push her tongue into my mouth.

Since I didn't want to take the girl into my pad, I led her along the High Street, then up Greenwich South Street, finally swinging right into Ash-burnham Place. A light drizzle was in the process of transforming itself into a downpour. When I opened up my umbrella, Vanessa used this as an excuse to huddle against me, taking hold of my arm although I'd not offered it to her. We walked to the end of the street, to the very heart of the Ashburnham Triangle, a quiet and highly desirable middle-class area bounded by the High Street, South Street and Blackheath Road. I swung left into Egerton Drive, then left again down Ashburnham Grove.

'Where are we going?' Holt demanded.

'We're not going anywhere,' I explained. 'I'm doing a bit of magick, that's all.'

We turned right once we were back on South Street, then right again down Devonshire Drive. We stopped to admire the former Roan School for Girls, a fine example of Victorian 'Gothic' design by Thomas Dinwiddy. After the school was merged with the Roan Boys School in 1984, the premises were left to rot for the best part of a decade. Then, having been denigrated to the status of artists' studios, the building was subsequently converted into quality apartment dwellings by Westcombe Homes. Having admired this top class piece of architecture, we wandered down to Holy Trinity and St Paul's Church on the corner of Egerton Drive. There is controversy among local historians over who designed the building, although it was officially opened as an Anglican church by William Milford Teulon, the Bishop of London, in 1866. After being left derelict for several years, the building had been bought and renovated by the Seventh Day Adventists.

'Come into the church,' a figure wreathed in a smile and smart casual wear beamed as we approached the portal, 'and get yourselves out of the rain.'

We followed our host into a reception room and as he didn't give any indication of leading us further into the church, I requested that we be shown the altar. While I took in the disagreeable fact that the seating for worship was made up of stacking chairs rather than pews, we were joined by another friendly face. One of the Adventists claimed that the church had been derelict for three years before they'd bought it, the other that it had lain unused for fifty. It was quite clear then neither of them knew anything of the building's history. The refurbishment was proficient but the clean lines and fresh plaster work were singularly lacking in atmosphere, making this newly renovated church the antithesis of the venues I was seeking out for my acts of sexual magick.

'Are you married?' the taller Adventist enquired.

'No,' I replied.

'You could get married in here,' the second Adventist ventured, 'but remember we hold our Sabbath services on Saturday, so it would have to be on a Sunday or during the week.'

'That would be nice, wouldn't it darling,' Vanessa said as she turned to me.

I made my excuses and left, with Holt pressing herself against me. I led the girl up Egerton Road, then down Guildford Grove and back on to Greenwich South Street. We ambled along to Blackheath Road and walked across the top of Egerton Drive, finally taking a right down Catherine Grove, which brought us back out on to Devonshire Drive, then taking two quick left turns, we walked along Greenwich High Street to Burgos Grove. This pleasant cul-de-sac was previously called Wellington Grove, but it was renamed in 1896 by some wags at the local council who thought it funny to commemorate the Iron Duke's only defeat, which took place in Spain in 1812.

We walked back along Greenwich High Street to Langdale Road and after traversing it, retired to the café in the train station for cappuccinos. I knew my magick was powerful and that it wouldn't be long before Vanessa presented me with an opportunity to complete the banishing ritual, of which our walk had formed the main act and all that awaited us was the denouement. While my companion perused a newspaper and consumed the piece of chocolate cake I'd bought for her, I studied the two waitresses. As well as serving customers, they were looking after a child. Both were wearing white blouses, short black skirts and black stockings, which showed their legs and arses to good effect. I preferred the slightly younger girl, who was in her mid-twenties with well-groomed shoulder length black hair. She caught the admiring glances I was throwing her way, and smiled several times.

'Do you love me?' Holt enquired as she looked up from a copy of the *Daily Mail*.

'Does a priest love the gods?' I replied cryptically.

'What is that supposed to mean?' Vanessa demanded.

'That we're going back to Payne's Wharf to do

some more sex magick!' I trumpeted to the entire café.

'What do you think I am?' Holt railed.

'To me,' I roared, 'you're just an archetype, the idea of woman without its substance, completely lacking any sense of the corporeal. As long as I think of you in that way, and simultaneously remember that you've been programmed with the personality of a truly wonderful young woman who was horribly murdered by your own father, then I can resist the desire I occasionally feel to imitate you as you ape the dead girl's behaviour!'

'You're mad!' Penelope lamented as she stormed off, thus proving the power of my magick. The banishing ritual had been a complete success.

I bought a take-out cappuccino, cursing the fact that it came in a foam cup as I made my way through the station. Everything went smoothly until I changed trains at Charlton, only to find that Penessa had mysteriously materialised on the platform. She sat next to me as we waited in a biting wind for the Gravesend train, and somehow managed to spill the dregs of my cappuccino over her gloves. When we got on the train, I instructed Brolt to place her mittens on the radiator, which was blasting out heat, so that they might dry out. I'd had enough of having my ear bent about the fact that they were wet. The journey was uneventful, although I must confess to feeling a certain psychic thrill as we passed through Abbey Wood.

Once we reached Gravesend, I led Penelope through the town centre and along to the ferry. I bought two day returns and Vanessa huddled against me as the ship crossed the Thames estuary. Penelope wanted to stop for a drink as we passed the World's End public house but I made her walk on to the fort. I paid for two guided tour tapes, then informed Vanessa that we were going to do everything backwards. I was determined to protect myself from the mind control techniques of English Heritage.

As the tapes we'd been handed began to relay information about the chapel and guard house, I forced Ness to inspect the underground magazines in the East Bastion. While the pre-recorded voice of the guide related the features of the West Bastion, we checked out the officers' barracks. By the time we were being blitzed with information about the powder magazines, we were looking over the north east bastion. And so it went on, with Penny complaining about the chill wind, her recriminations becoming increasingly bitter as we stood on the Landport gate to inspect the view across the inner and outer moats that protected the fort from the blasted heaths of Essex. Penessa wanted to borrow my gloves but I told her to keep her hands in her pockets, since these were far deeper than mine.

'What do you think?' Ness asked as we gazed across the flat Essex countryside.

'I'll levy soldiers with the coin they bring and chase the Prince of Parma from our land!'

'You'll what?' Penessa queried.

'Do you know nothing of your national history?' I chided. 'It was the defeat of the Spanish Armada in July 1588 that laid the foundation of the British

Empire. This was the bedrock from which John Dee made his most excellent conjurations, transforming Eliza into something far greater than simply a Virgin Queen, and thereby urging our nation along its imperial way!'

'I'm still not with you!' Penelope mewed.

'Elizabeth I paid her famous visit to Tilbury on 8 August 1588 in order to encourage one last effort from God's Englishmen! It was another nine days before the Duke of Parma withdrew his troops from the coast of the Low Countries!'

'What is this Christian rubbish?' Ness whinged.

I could see I was getting nowhere with the girl, so I led her through to the little museum in the powder magazines, where everything was explained on story boards, so that even the most simple of minds could follow this great narrative, the foundational myth of the very society I had vowed to destroy! After this, I led Penessa across the parade to the west bastion, where once again she complained about the freezing weather. In desperation, I took my companion into the brick chapel with its rubbed dressings, hipped tile roof and modillion cornice. There I made Penessa lie down on a pew, so that I might place her in a trance. This done, I questioned the wench about her past lives.

'The shore of the rocky island was so steep that we were within a crossbow shot of it in seven fathoms of water,' Ness droned. 'Then the ship struck the bottom, and split immediately, that is to say the lower part stuck fast and the upper parts were washed ashore, leaving the hulk level with the water, and only the castles and projecting parts visible, over which the sea broke so frequently and heavily that those who had taken refuge there were as much under water as those in the other parts of the ship, and thus each one clinging as best he could to the place where he chanced to find himself, the waves drove us ashore, while on all sides there arose a loud confusion of mournful cries, by which with one voice we called on our Lord for mercy.'

'Go on,' I urged as Penessa hesitated.

'And as most of the people had planks or barrels near them, or something similar by the help of which they hoped to swim ashore, as soon as the ship was under water those who trusted to that art began to throw themselves into the sea; but those who were not skilled in it and still remained in the ship, seeing that the mast drew them over and under water many times by the force of the heavy seas, determined to cut it away, for which purpose they cut the shrouds on the side of the sea and sent the mast overboard towards the land, to which they were so close that it almost touched dry ground. As each one was watching for the best opportunity to save himself, and the mast had the appearance of a bridge on which it seemed possible to reach the shore almost dry shod, thinking themselves saved, all those that could flung themselves upon it, covering it from end to end. But at that moment three or four heavy waves struck it and lifted it with such force that it shook off all those who were clinging to it, who were drawn under by the backward wash of the waves, till they struck the sail which was set upon the yard and spread out like a net, in which they were entangled, so that of all those who made the attempt, not one, alive or dead, reached land.'

'Don't stop!' I implored as there was another momentary break in the narrative.

'The sea was now covered with boxes, lances, barrels, and many other things which appeared in this mournful hour of shipwreck, floating in confusion with the people, most of whom were swimming ashore. It was a frightful thing to see and to relate the different sorts of torture which the fury of the sea inflicted on all, for everywhere there appeared some who could swim no farther to the last painful struggles with the water which was choking them; others, feeling their strength decrease, who commending themselves to the will of God, let themselves to the bottom for the last time; others who were wounded by the debris, or were stunned and let go their hold, were finished by the waves which dashed them upon rocks; others were wounded by the lances and nails in floating timbers, so that in many parts the colour of the water was red with blood from the wounds of those who thus ended their days.'

'Don't stop now!' I commanded.

'Meanwhile what remained of the ship parted in two pieces, the castles on one side and the poop on the other, upon which those who could not swim had taken refuge, not daring to commit themselves to the mast or the sea, seeing the disastrous fate of those who had attempted to reach the shore in either way. As soon as the ship was in two pieces, the sea could get a better hold of it, and the waves began to carry them ashore, tossing them from side to side, and thus now under, now above water, we drifted till it pleased our Lord that two or three large waves should cast the two pieces ashore, out of reach of the receding surf which had sucked them back several times, by means of which most of those who were left alive were saved.'

'What's going on here then?' a man from English Heritage enquired as he marched through the door.

'Nothing,' I said, 'nothing.'

Penessa woke from her trance and I led her from the fort to the World's End, where I ordered whisky on the rocks for both of us. The pub was a queer sort of place, and I felt less than welcome, sitting by a window well away from the locals who huddled at the bar. I remember a book dealer once telling me about some mighty strange goings on in Tilbury. This stout fellow was a direct descendent of Prince Henry St Clair of Normandy. Despite his noble blood, the book dealer had found the locals just as frosty as I did, but being in more rowdy company, he'd lasted longer than the single drink I managed.

When we got off the ferry at Gravesend, I took Penessa to Compton's, a working-class eatery near the river. It's one of those places where they make you pay ten pence for a sachet of brown sauce. Ness enjoyed her burger, while I made the mistake of ordering an omelette. We drank tea, which was good and strong, I'd never risk the coffee in one of those places. I enjoyed watching Penelope eat, she was beginning to put on weight. Give it a month or two and I'd no longer be able to see her cheek bones. Having consumed this repast, we made our way to the station. After changing trains at Charlton, we arrived back in Greenwich. Rather than going home, I took my companion into the Tai Won Mein. I ordered Mixed Vegetables with Noodles in Soup, while my double had Chicken Noodles.

Penelope claimed she wasn't hungry, but I made it clear I wouldn't pour her a glass of house red until she started to eat. The label claimed that Dun Huang only uses the world's classic grapes for its wines. In fact, it was Bulgarian wine that had been bottled in England, but for £6.80 you'd be very lucky to get anything better in a restaurant. As Ness polished off her food, I finished the Dun Huang and admired the menu. Although this was a Chinese restaurant, the menu was laid out in Japanese and English, presumably for the benefit of the many tourists who visited Greenwich. Penessa complained she'd eaten too much. After I made it clear that I'd only let her sleep with me if she threw up as I had my orgasm, Ness left in a huff. It had taken two attempts but the banishing ritual worked in the end.

Sayyida Nafisah met me at the airport, she'd driven while I'd taken the tube to Heathrow. After we'd both checked in, we went through passport control so that we could enjoy the hospitality of the duty-free pub. There, we drank rowdy toasts to tapsters, bezlors, carousers and wine-bibbers, bench-whistlers, lick-wimbles, down right drunkards, petty drunkards, bacchus boys, roaring boys, bacchanalians, tavern ancients, captains swaggers, fox-catchers, pot and half-pot men, quart, pint and half-pint men, short winded glass men, privy drunkards, half-pot companions and other good fellows of our fraternity.

'The beer drinker,' I announced after standing on a conveniently placed table, 'is mounted and *ale*-vated to such an *ale*-titude that he will talk of religion beyond belief, interpret the Scriptures beyond all sense and show you points of law above all reason that can be ale-edged!'

Those I'd been carousing with cheered heartily, while Sayyida dragged me to gate 32 since a final call for our flight had just been announced over the public address system. I fumbled with my seat-belt but needed the assistance of an air hostess to get it fastened. She was pretty, with bleached-blonde shoulder length hair and a muscular body which had been drenched in *Charlie* perfume. I mumbled something about the mile high club and she responded that for my own good, she would be unable to serve me my complimentary drinks. I fell asleep before the lights went off, allowing passengers to undo their seat-belts and light up. I felt much better, when after an exorbitant taxi ride, I gazed out across Lake Zurich. I breathed in the night air and knew that life was good.

I led my companion across the mouth of the Limmat, where looking to our left we had a view up the river, and to our right a view of the lake. Once we reached the right bank, I guided Nafisah into the old town. There was nothing I would have liked better than to have Sayyida watch as I lay with a whore in the market place, but unfortunately there was work to be done. Although I'd left the city more than eighty years previously, I experienced no difficulty in locating Spiegelgasse. On the way up to my old residence, I pointed out the dadaist club, where I'd spent many a pleasant night. I was glad to have lived further up the street, since the aspect it presents at the bottom end is particularly mean. We walked through two squares and then stopped. Still attached to the grill of a drain by a short chain, was the key I required.

'Come,' I said to Nafisah, 'there's nothing here but a few old memories, let us make our way to the left bank.'

I took my spirit guide through Grossmünster-platz, so that she might see the statue of Charlemagne. For reasons of security, I thought it best to remain silent about the significance of the building the statue adorned. If Sayyida was interested in religious reform, she would no doubt have heard of both Ulrich Zwingli and the towers which Victor Hugo sarcastically dismissed as 'pepper shakers'. By a twisting route, I led Nafisah back to the spot from which we had begun our journey. Taking a dollar bill from my pocket, I held this talisman above my head while simultaneously bidding the girl to follow six paces behind me as I led the way down the mile and a half length of Bahnhofstrasse, a shopping boulevard world famous for its lines of linden trees. The exquisite fashion stores, speciality houses, up-market jewellers and boutiques did not interest me. While the gourmet restaurants attracted my attention, my chief interest was the imposing banks and office buildings, since this is, after all, a prestige financial district. The stroll completed and the greenback having served its purpose, I burnt two thirds of the bill, then folded what remained of the talisman and placed it in a back pocket.

'The time is come!' I announced before leading Sayyida to a nondescript door.

I made good use of the key that I had left behind all those years ago. We walked into an elegantly furnished room and a closed circuit television camera monitored our progress as we made our way across to a leather three-piece suite that had provided many a weary traveller with some much welcome rest. We sat in silence for the best part of fifteen minutes, before a man came through and addressed us in French. He apologised for the delay, explaining that certain records had to be checked.

'No problem,' I assured him as I stood up.

As he led us through the heavily fortified building to a glass panelled lift, we exchanged small talk in a mixture of English, Italian, German and French. I said nothing to my angel as we plunged down into the bowels of the earth. Through the glass, we could see a glistening array of art treasures, many of them stolen from their rightful owners by Hitler and his henchmen during the last inter-imperialist war. The lift halted and we wandered through rooms piled high with priceless baubles. Eventually, we reached our destination. A door was thrown open, revealing a chamber piled high with silver and gold ingots, old master paintings and vintage wines.

'These are your Russian holdings,' our guide announced in perfect BBC English, 'I trust sir finds everything in order.'

'Everything looks fine, I just wanted my companion to see a fraction of my reserves, having done so, I'm happy to go.'

Naturally, I'd booked a room in the Hotel Savoy since I appreciated the crisp linen and excellent room service. Having re-emerged from the vaults, Sayyida and I made our way directly there. I ordered sandwiches and a night-cap, five minutes after consuming this modest fare I was in bed. I went out like a light and woke at dawn to find Nafisah tugging at my morning glory. There wasn't time for full sex, so the girl wanked me off. As the babe worked my meat, and love juice boiled up through my groin, I tried to remember where the hell I'd met the girl. Through the haze of my hangover, I surmised that my dirty pudding was an aspiring actress in search of a bit part.

A taxi got us to the airport with very little time to spare. My companion made cryptic comments about changes in my mood throughout the journey, which she claimed to look upon as some sort of occult test. Despite finding this conceit, which I considered to be a rather miserable attempt at method-acting, rather silly, I persuaded the thespian to drive me to Farringdon once we'd negotiated our way through immigration control at Heathrow. I must confess to being rather worried about finding myself in possession of a passport that bore my photograph and somebody else's name. Nevertheless, I thought it expedient to make use of this forgery rather than admitting I'd misplaced the genuine documents.

Although I wouldn't say that I was early, neither was I late. Vanessa Holt was perched elegantly on one of the wooden benches in the Quality Chop House when I walked through its portal. For the starter, the starlet ordered Artichoke Vinaigrette, while I had Warm Asparagus with Pecorino. I liked my lunch companion's appearance and I quickly concluded that she'd been to the same drama school as my dirty stop-over in Zurich, since both were working through the same method-acting fantasy about occult initiation.

'I burn, I blaze, I am consumed, wretch that I am, by the evils that possess me,' the wanton announced as I poured her a second glass of Cremant de Bourgogne '93.

I was glad that I'd chosen a venue that prides itself on quality and civility for my lunch date with this slightly maladjusted young lady. The Quality Chop House styles itself as a 'progressive working-class caterer,' and the waitress was a gem who pretended this conversational gambit was quite normal as she dished up Vanessa's Steak Tartar with chips and my Roast Vegetables with Goat's Cheese Salad. The food was cooked to perfection, and the service excellent, making for a relaxed atmosphere where eccentric conversations weren't frowned upon as long as they were conducted in a civil fashion that didn't intrude upon the privacy of other dinners.

'Come, rattle-head,' I said as I extended an arm across the table and ruffled the girl's hair, 'you've been keeping the company of shallow-patted hair-brained shittle-witted coxcombes who display little regard for either law or religion. Forget about building castles in the air, let's order pudding and I'll show you a novel use for crème brûlée.'

'If I didn't know the power of your sex-magick,' Joanna retorted, 'I'd accuse you of being sexually obsessed!'

After exchanging banter of this type for several minutes, it became obvious that Susan didn't want a one-night stand, she was looking for a husband. In the end, I ordered a caramel cheesecake, while my companion choose a sorbet. We finished the meal with cappuccinos, and I was overcome by a feeling of bonhomie as we made our way on to the street.

'Where are you living?' Miranda demanded.

'I forget,' was my retort.

'I want to see your town house and a recent bank statement,' Felicity pouted.

'If you don't want to screw me,' I snarled, 'will you watch while a common prostitute and I make the beast with two backs?'

'Certainly not,' Sonia cried as she hailed a taxi.

For some reason I was pleased as the black cab disappeared in the direction of King's Cross. I felt as if I'd met the girl in some other life and that then as now, her presence had been a great burden to me. I wandered down towards Farringdon tube, then wondered where the hell I was going. Rather than taking the underground, I strode purposefully along Farringdon Road but I stopped in my tracks when I took in St John's Gate. The Knights of St John had been the principal beneficiaries of the suppression of the Templars, taking over many of the properties belonging to the disgraced order. In England, the Hospitallers had been suppressed after the reformation, but revived again in a Protestant guise during the Victorian era. I was in two minds about what to do next, whether I should visit the Museum of the Order of St John or take a look at the Grand Priory Church across the street.

I tottered on the edge of the curb and was nearly run down by a bus. Visions of being whisked off to some isolated hospital by members of the St John's ambulance brigade flashed through my mind. Much as I wanted to view the Flemish triptych in the museum, I wondered if doing so was taking too much of a risk. Likewise, the Grand Priory Church had a circular nave, something suspiciously close to Templar motifs. Taking discretion to be the better part of valour, I decided to retrace my steps, until it suddenly struck me that this might also be considered somewhat Satanic. As I stood rooted to the spot, a man dressed in a black suit approached me.

'The true Principles of things,' he announced, 'are produced out of the four elements in the following manner. Nature, whose power is in her obedience to the Will of God, ordained from the very beginning, that the four elements should incessantly act on one another, so, in obedience to her behest, fire began to act on air, and produced Sulphur. Air acted on water and produced Mercury. Water, by its action on Earth, produced Salt. Earth, alone, having nothing to act upon, did not produce anything, but became the nurse, or womb, of these three Principles. We designedly speak of three Principles, for though the Ancients mention only two, it is clear that they omitted the third, Salt, not from ignorance, but from a desire to lead the uninitiated astray.'

'Go, Belimoth, go!' I screamed at the phantom.

There was a screeching of tyres, and a howling of police sirens. The traffic halted and a fiery Angel appeared in the sky. I raised my arms in a gesture of supplication and a blinding light flooded the pavement with its reflective brilliance. The clouds broke into two warring factions, making themselves into the figures of a Lion and a Knight in Armour respectively. The Knight sheaved his sword and wrestled his beastly opponent with his bare hands. The Lion snapped viciously at this figure, but my champion was nimble enough to evade these deadly jaws. Eventually, the Lion conceded defeat by lying on his back with all four paws sticking straight up in the air. The stranger who had molested me, melted away and somehow I found the strength to make my way to the Barbican.

# SIX

I CLOSED MY EYES and relaxed, when I opened them again Sayyida Nafisah had disappeared but a man I recognised as Dr Kevin Callan was sitting opposite me. He was my controller, the man from whom it felt as if I'd spent a lifetime trying to escape. I followed Callan to his car and he drove me to his office in Belgravia.

'You look tired,' Callan said sympathetically, 'you need a vitamin shot.'

'I don't want to kill him,' I sobbed as I was strapped to the operating table, 'I really don't want to stab him.'

'You don't have any choice,' the doctor told me as he swabbed my arm, 'you thought you'd broken our cycle of control but we've programmed every episode of this sorry saga.'

'I don't understand.'

'This is the next stage of our mind control experiment,' the surgeon explained, 'we want to teach our patients to consciously activate different personalities we've programmed into them, so that they can make the most of any situation they encounter during the course of their espionage activities.'

'It's not a natural part of my make-up to commit murder!' I wailed.

'Nonsense,' Callan snapped, 'have you no grasp of the mechanism of mimetic desire?'

'No,' I replied.

'We value objects,' the doctor explained, 'because other people desire them. We learn this system of value by imitating other people, we don't so much desire objects as desire to be like other people. But wanting what other people want leads to conflict. To bring conflict to an end there has to be a surrogate, a sacrificial victim, a final killing to bring order into society. You've been programmed with a personality that is identical to the one we've implanted in the mind of Philip Sloane's double. This will necessarily lead to conflict between you and the film-maker, a conflict that you will only be able to resolve through his sacrifice!'

'It's horrible,' I moaned, 'it's too horrible!'

'No it's not,' Callan insisted, 'it's an act that will justify all the funds that have been poured into my research! No matter how hard you try to resist, in the end you will do my bidding!'

'No I won't!' I protested as I felt a needle being slipped into my vein, and after that I can remember nothing more for what might be anything between several hours and several weeks.

I slept and then I woke and eventually I made my

way back to Brick Lane. Sayyida was in the flat and she poured me a shot of William Grant's family reserve finest Scotch whisky, blended and bottled in Scotland by an independent company for five generations. Nafisah opened various kitchen cupboards but they were virtually bare. There was a tin of baked beans but no bread, it seemed pointless eating at home. Instead, we made our way to the Clifton Balti House on the corner of Brick Lane and Hanbury Street, the later road being the site of one of the notorious Jack The Ripper murders. The restaurant was a little crowded but the service was good and the food excellent.

'A real Balti!' Sayyida exclaimed as she tucked into her chicken curry. 'A proper Balti is served in the dish it was cooked in, it's a joke when you go into an Indian restaurant only to find the dish your hot Balti has been served in is cold!'

'Look,' I said as I used a spoon to make an excavation into my Korma, 'this is the real test that the food has been cooked in the dish, the coloration around the edge should be different at the top and the bottom. This one passes.'

'You're right,' Nafisah confirmed, 'and mine passes with flying colours too.'

'Tastes good!' I yelped as I tore a strip from my nan and dipped it into the Korma.

I could feel myself getting an erection as Sayyida slopped a piece of nan around her dish, then shoved the princely delicate into her O-shaped open mouth. I imagined the way Nafisah's breasts and stomach would swell up if she was placed on a regime of forced feeding. I visualised her huge arse, the love handles spilling over the top of her Levi jeans, her massive thighs and arms. The girl had put on weight since I'd first met her, but she was too skinny, far too skinny. Although her size fourteen clothes were looking a little tight, she wasn't ready to make the leap to sixteen, something I most earnestly desired to see.

'Penny for your thoughts?' Sayyida whispered.

'Thunderbird,' I shot back, 'Thunderbird.'

'Oh, yeah,' Natasha grinned, 'I've gotta get you some more Thunderbird. You've been away for weeks, it's all so mysterious. I never know where you've been or when you're coming back. Anyway, I hope the Grant's was okay, I would have got 100 Pipers but they didn't have any in the supermarket. I drank the Thunderbird last night and haven't got around to replacing it.'

'Don't worry,' I mumbled, 'just eat, eat!'

'I feel stuffed!' Sayyida confessed as she patted the beginnings of a pot belly.

'But you're so skinny!' I screeched. 'You must eat everything up and then I'll buy you a pudding.'

I could have spent another hour in bed since I couldn't get a cheap day return until nine-thirty. I'd got up anyway and put two slices of wholemeal in the toaster. I was listening to the travel report on the radio when the phone rang.

'Hello.'

'Is that Mr Sloane?'

'Yes.'

'Jahbulon!'

'Jahbulon?'

I put the phone down and poured the coffee I'd brewed into the sink, threw away the toast which was now ready, slipped on a jacket, picked up a raincoat and my briefcase. I was ready to hit the road. As I was locking the door, I realised the radio was still blaring. I went back inside and switched it off. The walk to Turnham Green tube station usually took five minutes but I did it in three. A train pulled in as I rushed along the platform, district line to Upminster. I must have bought a paper at Victoria, since I remember glancing through it on the train.

'Mr Sloane?'

It was Sister George, I turned around to face her. She was a littler older than me but still in her thirties. Her white uniform was dazzling in the bright sunlight.

'Yes.'

'I, I had no choice... your father... your mother...' Sister George stammered.

'Mr Sloane?' It was Dr James Braid.

'Yes.'

'I want a word, could you come with me.'

I followed the doctor out into the corridor, then into an empty ward where he told me to sit down on a bed. I don't remember what the doctor said, we exchanged a few words and then I was back in the ward with Sister George.

I fell asleep and Sister George came by and put the oxygen mask over my face. I don't recall exactly what happened next, maybe she was taking my pulse or maybe she was just holding my hand.

'Can you get me something to eat?'

'You need a break.' Dr Braid observed, 'Maybe you should go out and get something yourself.'

It took about five minutes to walk to a fast food outlet, where I bought a pizza and a can of coke. I consumed this fare as I made my way back to the hospital. When I reached Dr Braid's office a nurse informed me he'd been called out unexpectedly. I sat down and leafed through the paper, taking in a little more of the news than I'd managed on the train. When I woke up, I pulled the oxygen mask from my face and tried to speak. Sister George took my hand, or maybe she was taking my pulse. A passing nurse tried to put the oxygen mask back on but Sister George motioned her to leave me alone.

Sister George called out to a doctor, exchanged a few words with him and then led me out of the ward. She took me up to another floor and left me sitting alone. She came back ten minutes later with a pot of tea and some biscuits. Sister George didn't stay long. Once she'd gone, I poured myself a cup of tea and dunked a biscuit into the brew. Another nurse gave me a paper chit and several plastic bags filled with my possessions. Sometime later, a different nurse came in with some forms and instruction booklets. I took these and put them in my briefcase.

I poured another cup of tea and drank it when the nurse went. I stared out of the window and although it was still light, I can't remember anything about the view. The first nurse came back and asked if I wanted to say goodbye to Sister George and Dr Braid. After I'd said that I did, she led me back down to the ward.

After that, I guess I must have gone to the nearest pub, I can't recall what it was called. I ordered a pint of Guinness, drank it, ordered another and then sat down at an unoccupied table. It must have been about seven o'clock on Friday night but there weren't many drinkers in the boozer. After finishing my second pint I made my way to the Gents. As I was pissing into a urinal a middle-aged man came in and stood beside me.

'We're lucky to be here,' he announced, 'I've a friend who's in hospital with a broken leg. He was run down, it could have been either of us!'

'I've just come from the hospital,' I raved. 'The doctor there tells me I've had my old personality stripped away and replaced by one of his choosing.'

'Come on, I'll buy you a drink,' the geezer coaxed.

'I don't want another drink, I've had two already.'

'Yes you do, you need to get drunk,' the stranger said as he tried to put both his arms around me.

'Leave me alone!' I yelled as I pushed him away.

The man grabbed my shoulder as I made my way towards the door. I turned around and punched him in the face. He staggered backwards and slid to the floor. The last thing I remember is him sitting there holding his nose, with blood bubbling up from beneath his fingers and a look of shocked surprise in his eyes.

I woke up in a strange bed. I didn't know what time it was. There wasn't anyone beside me. I got up and drew the curtains. I was looking out over row upon row of terraces. There wasn't much in the bedroom except for a weird selection of clothes and some surrealist prints on the wall. According to an alarm clock it was ten, since it was dark I concluded this meant pm. I found my companion in the main room, drinking a bottle of 100 Pipers. There was a wall of books behind her. I scanned the spines, works by Ernst Bloch, Georg Lukács and Theodor Adorno amongst others. The titles of their books made it plain that these authors wrote in a highly theoretical manner, as did the fact that the handful of names which meant anything to me all belonged to famous Marxists. Among the later were Walter Benjamin, Bertolt Brecht and Herbert Marcuse. I closed my eyes, reached out and pulled a book from a shelf. This turned out to be *Dialectical Materialism* by Henri Lefebvre, which at that time appeared completely incomprehensible to my untutored eyes.

'Do you think I'm sexy?' Sayyida was sloshed, her speech was slurred. 'Or in your opinion am I just highly intelligent?'

'I'm turned on by intelligence!' I retorted.

'What kind of intelligence?' Nafisah demanded. 'British? American? Israeli?'

'British is best!' I replied patriotically.

Perhaps not the most auspicious start to a conversation, but not inauspicious when you consider that I'd slept with Sayyida on the odd occasion when we'd both been pissed. As I eased myself on to the sofa beside Nafisha, she brushed her hand against my leg. Going back to her place would be infinitely preferable to staying in a British intelligence safe house. Although I wanted to start clearing the place out, I had the whole of Sunday ahead of me with nothing else to do, so a few hours of pleasure in the meantime wasn't asking much.

After sharing what remained of the 100 Pipers, we went to bed about four in the morning. Once we were both undressed, I got on top of Sayyida and just slipped inside her. There was no foreplay, or if there was, it had taken place in the living room where we'd spent several hours dancing. Sayyida lay on the bed like a beached whale, too drunk to make me very interested in giving her a good time. I decided not to hold back and after two or three minutes of fucking I'd shot my load. I rolled off my partner and she quickly fell asleep. I lay awake beside her, when she started snoring I decided to get up. My movement woke her, she sat up and grabbed my arm.

'Michael,' the girl cried as she pulled me towards her, 'are you alright?'

'My name's not Michael,' I spluttered, 'it's Peter.'

'This is mad,' my companion shot back, 'a couple of weeks ago I ran into you on Greenwich Church Street and you claimed your name was Stephen. What's more, I had to tell you I was called Sayyida, since you insisted we'd never met before.'

'What happened?' I demanded.

'I suppose it was some sort of test,' Nafisah confessed. 'You took me back to a flat that you insisted was your only home, despite the fact that I'd been to your pad in Brixton, as well as your summer camp-site by the West Kennet Long Barrow.'

'Could you find the camp-site again?' I enquired.

'No problem,' Sayyida replied, 'it's very close to the Avebury stone circle.'

Despite our early start, the traffic was already snarling up over Tower Bridge, and it was a night-mare getting down to the Elephant and Castle. From there we cut through several back streets, but ended up crawling along from Clapham to Weybridge. We'd have probably been better off staying north of the river and heading out of town via Hammersmith! We stopped at Marlborough to get something to eat and look at the famous public school that takes its name from the town. I informed Nafisha that this was where I'd been educated, although I don't think she believed me. We passed through Hungerford, site of the famous Michael Ryan massacre and motored peacefully on to Avebury.

We parked in the tourist car park with its rotting wooden fencing, then walked through the village. As we made our way around the huge stone circle, I felt a strong connection to the primal Truths of our ancestors' fertility religions. Sayyida and I wound our way around the top of the huge earth works that greatly added to the psychogeographical intensity of this Neolithic site. Looking out across the grass plains spread before us, there an unending vista of green that eventually merged with the grey of a stormy sky. The stones themselves are of two distinct types, tall column-shaped stones representing the male, and squat megaliths that had been hewn into a diamond-like cut to symbolise the female, with the man-made oval of Silbury Hill representing that most desirable of objects, the pregnant woman.

Having made our way around the stone circle that encloses the village, we cut along the West Kennet Avenue, with its procession of megaliths and marker posts to indicate where stones have been destroyed by Christian vandals. Here, the mysteries of life and death were once confronted in a manner remarkably similar to the rites of Aztecs on another continent. The ancient Britons and the Celts were not afraid of death, they'd face it bravely in voluntary acts of ritual human sacrifice. As I walked, my forgetting of everything I knew about Philip Sloane, a programmed personality whose avant-garde films were a worthless sham, was simultaneously an act of remembrance. It was my privilege to be the nameless stranger who'd given up all worldly concerns to become High Priest to the Sun. I was consorting with Mother Earth, out of whose dark belly everything joyous and fruitful sprang.

'Having considered terror as producing an unnatural tension and certain violent emotions of the nerves,' I announced to a startled Nafisah. 'Whatever is fitted to produce such a tension must be productive of a passion similar to terror, and consequently must be a source of the sublime.'

'The whole of this doctrine leads us to a conclusion, which is of great importance in the present affair,' Vanessa rejoined. 'Viz, that all the nice and subtle questions concerning personal identity can never possibly be decided, and are to be regarded rather as grammatical than as philosophical difficulties. Identity depends on the relations of ideas, and these relations produce identity, by means of that easy transition they occasion.'

'Bollocks!' I spat.

'All the disputes concerning the identity of connected objects are merely verbal,' Penessa was really pressing home the point. 'Except in so far as the relation of parts gives rise to some fiction or imaginary principle of union, as I have already observed.'

'Get thee to a Nunnery gone!' I yelled whilst simultaneously making the sign of the five-pointed star rising in the East.

The air around Holt shimmered and soon after the banshee was gone, to be replaced, as was my want, with a milder mannered elemental. It was at this point that the course of the avenue took us on to a rough country road. Our conversation ceased as Nafisah fell in several paces behind me. My willingness to observe the customs of her culture as regards relations between the sexes, clearly filled the girl with joy. From here, we followed the course of the road, turning right when we reached West Kennet. We passed some country cottages, then crossed the road and made our way down a track to a babbling brook. The water made me feel the full strength of my connection to Nature, as did the country air as we cut along the edge of a field. We climbed a gate, then turned sharp left, making

our way up the track that led directly to the Long
Barrow.

'Oh shrieking beloved brother blockheads of
Mankind,' Sayyida ululated as I led her to the brow
of the hill, 'let us close those wide mouths of ours,
let us cease our shrieking and submit to the Will of
God!'

'You mean the gods,' I corrected.

Rather than taking Nafisah straight into the burial
chambers, I took her hand and ascended the mound.
We walked its length, when we stopped at the far
end, Sayyida turned and kissed me. We embraced, I
held Beth tight against me. The wind whistled
around us, we were all alone in a wilderness of our
own making. I broke the embrace and made my way
back along the brow of the mound, Ness followed
me.

'I'm ready for anything,' she announced.

'Come search the corpses then,' my words drifted
off into time and space, both of which died yes-
terday and will die again tomorrow, so that time
may cease and midnight never come.

We made our way into the womb. Sayyida threw
off her clothes, then slowly, teasingly, undressed me.
Finally, we stood completely naked, my erect prick
a finger pointing towards eternity. These eight inches
of swollen flesh were a triumph of human imagination, that special combination of intellection and
passion, the zeroes and ones of a world without
beginning or end. Nafisah leapt at me, and as she
clawed my flesh, I wrestled her to the ground. Eve
was lying on her back, so I flipped my assailant on

to her stomach and pressed myself against her. We were covered in mud and I took delight in spreading more of this filth over Penessa's breasts while pressing them firmly beneath my palms.

'Fuck me! FUCK ME!' Caroline bellowed.

'Some who allow darkness to be a cause of the sublime,' I boomed as I rubbed mud around Tracy's juicy clit, 'would infer from the dilation of the pupil, that a relaxation may be productive of the sublime as well as a convulsion. However, although the circular ring of the iris be in some sense a sphincter, which may possibly be dilated by a simple relaxation, yet in one respect it differs from most of the other sphincters of the body, that it is furnished with antagonist muscles, which are the radial fibres of the iris, no sooner does the circular muscle begin to relax, than these fibres wanting their counterpoise, are forcibly drawn back, and open the pupil to a considerable wideness.'

As I said this, I thrust my cock into Sandra's black hole of a cunt and bit viciously into her right shoulder. Denise then let rip with a great scream of pleasure and I could feel her body shuddering beneath me as multiple orgasms wracked her bulk. I could feel love juice being drawn up through my groin, and it wasn't long before this spurted into that chasm that unites both life and death. For a long time, I lay panting on top of Louise. An unholy union of Earth Mother and the Sun.

After a tedious drive through the dark, we arrived back at Spitalfields. Having parked the car, we retired to the Nazrul on Brick Lane. In many ways, with its red flock wallpaper and mirroring, this is a very traditional Indian restaurant. However, the wooden tables are bare rather than being covered with a cloth, so the place has the relaxed atmosphere of a working man's café. After kicking off with papadoms and a chutney tray, I ordered the Vegetable Rogon Josh with pilau rice and garlic nan. Sayyida had Chicken & Prawn Dhansak with special fried rice and pashwari nan. Since the restaurant wasn't licensed, I was drinking Mango Lachee while Nafisah had a coke.

'Hieroglyphically,' I announced as Sayyida ate, 'Beth, the second Hebrew letter, expresses the mouth of our species as the organ of speech. Speech is the production of our inner self. Therefore Beth expresses that inner self, central as a dwelling, to which one can retire without fear of disturbance. From this idea arises that of a Sanctuary, an inviolate abode for man and for God. But Beth also expresses every production that emanates from this mysterious retreat, every internal activity, and from it issue ideas of instruction, of the higher Knowledge, of Law, of Erudition, of Occult Science or Kabbalah.'

'But how would you relate this to the literary productions of writers such as Raymond Queneau and Harry Matthews, who belong to the Oulipo group?' Jenny demanded.

'Always,' I announced, 'these poltroons will be loathsome and repugnant and hateful to us, for they have plundered the fifth letter of our alphabet with terrible hand!'

I ordered coffee and drank it hurriedly, because by the time it arrived I'd decided that what I really wanted was a drink. I led Sayyida south down Brick Lane, then cut west along Church Street. This desirable road was developed in the early part of the eighteenth century. Although the houses had been built for wealthy merchants, they were quickly adapted to the use of artisans and lost their purely domestic function. Today, the street accommodates a number of arrivistes, who nobody in their right mind would want as a neighbour. Christ Church, Hawksmoor's greatest achievement, stood on one corner of the junction with Commercial Street. On the other side was the Ten Bells pub, an old haunt of mine. I decided it was better not to take Nafisah inside, since someone might relish the opportunity of regaling the girl with tales of the feminist protests that had been staged outside the boozery in the nineteen-eighties.

Instead, we negotiated Commercial Street with the aid of a conveniently placed pelican crossing. We cut across Brushfield Street, with Spitalfields Market looming above us to our right, and headed straight for The Gun. This is a traditional boozery with a somewhat down-market clientele. The carpet was perhaps the most outstanding feature, since it was patterned with the repeated motif of a cannon. There was the odd gun on the wall, along with a plethora of prints all dedicated to military themes. Mugs and glasses were also hung from rings on the walls, looking for all the world as if they were never used.

'Two pints of lager and a packet of crisps please,' I said to the barmaid when it was my turn to be served.

'What flavour?' she demanded.

'Cheese and onion,' I shot back without a moment's hesitation.

Having secured our flagons, I was somewhat miffed to discover all the seats were taken. This meant standing up, a function I've never associated with really serious drinking. After consuming a pint, I decided to cut my losses and show Nafisah the digs where I'd had an incredible night of passion with a right little raver called Marie-Jeanette, a good Catholic girl she was, whose surname I've forgotten. When I was younger, I certainly knew how to show a girl a good time! The area had changed a great deal since I'd last visited, Dorset Street being completely demolished. Since I was unable to show my consort the now legendary site of my revelry, I led her into the multi-storey car park that had been built over it. Once we were in a badly lit corner, I took a twenty-pound note from my pocket and shoved it between Sayyida's breasts.

'You treat me like a prostitute,' my disciple complained.

'Am I your pimp or a punter!' I hooted.

Nafisah unzipped my flies, seconds later my cock was hardening in her hand. She looked at my erection, then looked me in the eye, and we both knew the answer to my question. I could feel the old urges welling up inside me, but I managed to resist them as Sayyida worked my member in a steady rhythm. Not yet, the time was not right, there were many things to be sorted out before Nafisah would be called upon to become the ultimate sacrifice. I looked at the girl and imagined her six months from hence, with a swollen belly and huge breasts. I had to feed her up before she could return from whence she'd come. I could feel my back stiffening as Sayyida increased the speed with which she worked my meat. My seed splattered against concrete, wasted but not wasted, since the night was still young.

After we left the car park, I took Nafisah to the nearest Halal fried chicken shop, where I bought her a burger and chips. On the drive to Greenwich, I was popping the chips into Sayyida's mouth and making her eat them. I took this Goddess back to my safe-house on Church Street and fed her ice cream and lager. After she'd protested that she was feeling sick, I told her sickness was an important element of her magickal instruction. Nafisah stopped complaining and I had a vision of her belly swelling up. Once Sayyida was groaning under the strain of what I'd made her consume, I loaded the few possessions I wanted into the car and insisted she take me back to Brick Lane.

'I'm not well enough to drive,' Nafisah complained.

'That's the whole point,' I insisted.

Sayyida slipped the car into gear and headed for the Blackwall Tunnel. We were crawling along, so I made Nafisah press her foot hard against the accelerator. I had to think on my feet, issuing the girl with a constant stream of instructions, since a certain amount of pressure had to be applied if we were going to avoid involvement in a serious road accident. We arrived and I took my things up to my new flat, leaving Sayyida slumped over the wheel of her Fiesta. When I came down to fetch her up, she was puking into her own lap.

'Come on,' I yelped. 'Come on. I'm not putting up with this kind of nonsense, I'm not going to allow one of my disciples to develop an eating disorder. If you throw up your food, you'll just have to consume another meal.'

'Oh, no. Oh no!' Nafisah groaned.

'Oh yes!' I insisted. 'And you are to eat all your greens too!'

As it turned out, I was out of vegetables, so I opened a tin of rice pudding and fed Sayyida that instead. There wasn't any booze in the house and I didn't know where to get any at that time of night. To make up for this, I nipped out to the twenty-four-hour bakery, where I bought my guest bagels and an assortment of cakes.

# ✥ SEVEN ✥

VANESSA HOLT CALLED ON me at my room above the Slug and Lettuce public house on Shoreditch High Street. I hadn't given her the address and I don't know where she'd obtained it. I had another room in Brick Lane, which was where my followers were supposed to search me out if they were in desperate need of spiritual guidance. Vanessa didn't like the shared kitchen and toilet. In fact, she thoroughly disliked my room, which was strewn with clothes, papers and books. I made some tea and Holt complained because I'd run out of milk.

'How can you live like this?' Vanessa demanded.

'Do you think I shit like everyone else?' was my cryptic retort.

'Yes I do!' Penessa insisted.

'Well fuck you!' I sparred as I brought my features within an inch of the doppelagänger's face.

'You're not fucking me!' Penelope snapped. 'I'm sick of being treated like a prostitute!'

'You love it, doll,' I puttered while simultaneously grabbing my tormentor's tit and squeezing it gently.

As Vanessa slapped my face, I could feel myself falling back through fields of rape. Things were spinning and I was dizzy with excitement. I'd been exploring the astral plane for some time but to meet somebody else there proved that it was more than a mere psychological projection on the part of individual occultists, it was proof positive that the spirit world had an objective existence. I hurried along Redchurch Street, crossed Bethnal Green Road and ran into my double at the corner of Brick Lane.

'We exist!' Penelope cried in triumph.

'And therefore we are but shadows!' was my exaltation.

I took the girl by the hand, led her across Bethnal Green Road and on to the Boundary Estate. The delightful red brick blocks of flats that surrounded us had been erected by London County Council in 1900 on the site of the notorious 'Old Nichol' slum, they were an early and highly successful experiment in municipal housing. We traversed the tiny tiered park in Arnold Circus, then made our way down Calvert Avenue. As we passed St Leonard's, I pointed out the Shoreditch village stock and whipping post in the churchyard.

'Would you like to whip me?' Penessa enquired.

'Oh yes!' I replied. 'I'd like to tan your hide with a bundle of wet thorns!'

'How predictable!' Holt teased. 'You're such a macho bore, if you had any subtlety you'd prefer birch twigs.'

'I much prefer birch twigs,' I harangued, 'but one has to make concessions if the symbols of the spiritual life are to be correctly directed to our higher ends.'

'Don't you ever listen to me?' Vanessa raved. 'You're a sexist pig! Do you think Jesus sucked cock? Do you think He was having it away with John The Baptist, or was He giving Mary Magdalene a shafting?'

'What's wrong with you?' I requisitioned. 'Can't you see I'm only interested in Mary's role as Theotokos?'

'You can stuff your Mariolatry, I'm not interested in Mary Tudor when we could be discussing Good Queen Bess!'

'You drink too much, that's your problem. The pubs aren't even open and already you want a vodka!'

'The rose makes honey for the bees,' Vanessa warranted.

'Rosicrucian nonsense,' I chortled.

In this fashion, we made our way up Kingsland Road to the Geffrye Museum. Here an aggregation of English domestic interiors are housed in what were once the Geffrye Almshouses, homes for pensioners and widows built by the Ironmongers' Company at the beginning of the eighteenth century. We wandered along the corridor that had been knocked through what were once separate homes. The Tudor interiors were just about bearable, although to my eyes the dark woods and rush mats would have become somewhat oppressive if I'd had to live with them once the dark nights drew in. As the 'English' identity and character became established on an increasingly firm footing, the displays of drawing room furniture grew completely unbearable. I thought the Victorian era was the pits, until I saw the room representing the 1930s. We had to go upstairs to find the light at the end of the tunnel, fifties furniture and fires with a space age glow. The allied 'victory' in World War II was achieved at the expense of the British Empire, and this together with the cosmopolitan benefits of mass immigration from the West Indies, broke through the dam of repressions holding together English character armour.

'Yes, yes!' I whooped as Vanessa drank in the bold lines and noble simplicity of the fifties. 'This is where we must project ourselves for our first astral sex session!'

Deliriously happy, we made a hasty exit from the museum and soon found ourselves wandering down Shoreditch High Street. It had once been the centre of the furniture industry but now there were thousands of wholesalers packed into the district, not to mention shops specialising in ladies fashions. I bought Vanessa some trinkets and a dress, then we had a meal in the Market Cafe on Church Street. The orange interior and traditional working-class fare were not really to my taste. The Radio Two twitterings that filled the room gave one the feeling that the establishment existed in a time warp somewhere around 1946. The double egg and chips I ordered was a mistake, it lay heavily on my stomach, adding to my feelings of estrangement.

Normally, I would have enjoyed watching Holt eat but a very peculiar sensation came over me. While we'd been shopping I'd taken an extraordinarily keen interest in Vanessa's purchases. Indeed, I'd felt rather hurt that the stores we'd visited didn't have clothes in my size. At the cafe, I'd ordered the same food as my companion and found myself copying every gesture she made. I was even downing hot chocolate, one of Vanessa's favourite tipples.

Holt was scratching her head, and I was scratching mine too, it was like looking in a mirror. Vanessa obviously thought I was behaving strangely, so she slapped her wrist and then began feeling her breast to see if I copied these gestures, which I did. Next, Holt made her way to the ladies' loo in Spitalfields Market, I followed closely on her heels. My companion disappeared into a cubicle and I was about to make my way into the one next to this, when I caught a glimpse of myself in a mirror. Last time I'd looked at myself I didn't have long hair and a fair-sized pair of knockers. Finally, I spontaneously re-experienced a spiritual exercise I'd long ago performed under the tutelage of a Sufi master, which entails visualising one's own body being hacked to pieces. It was certainly me who was quartered during the course of my hallucination, but in the vision I'd taken on Vanessa's female form.

'Are you okay?' Holt was leaning over me splashing cold water in my face.

'I think so?' I whispered, completely unsure about who I was.

Vanessa helped me up. I just wanted to go to my room above the Slug and Lettuce, where I could place the pillow case with the single eye-hole cut into it over my head, so that I could pretend I was a Ling master. Nafisah had something else on her mind. She led me to a bench, where we sat down.

'You have to understand,' Sayyida explained, 'that as a black woman, I experience everything three times, that rather than having a homogenised experience of the world, I possess triple consciousness. The dominant reality is constructed by white males, who like me are English. I've absorbed the same ideological structures into my consciousness as every other "Englishman", and I experience reality through these constructs. But as a Muslim and a woman, I am systematically discriminated against in my everyday life. Therefore, I experience reality simultaneously twice more, through a matrix of oppression constructed around race and another structured around gender.'

I sat down on a bench on the South Bank of the Thames, directly opposite the Houses of Parliament. Last time I'd deposited myself on the same seat, a dozen years earlier, a rozzer had attempted to get fresh with me. This time my possible appointment was with Dr James Braid and it wasn't long before he appeared through the sun-swizzled riverscape. Braid looked pale, the black bags under his eyes were a sign of the intense pressure he was under to justify the funding for his mind control experiments.

'How do,' Braid only used northern lingo when he was sloshed or stressed.

'Your daughter is a lousy lay,' I complained, 'she just lies lifelessly beneath me doing sweet FA whenever we make love. Even if I tell her to grab my balls or run her nails down my back, Penelope carries out my instructions in an utterly mechanical fashion. The bitch is completely lacking in sexual imagination, and to top it all, she's a shrew!'

The doctor sat down beside me and stared blankly across the river towards Westminster, while simultaneously unbuttoning his coat and removing a flagon of 100 Pipers Scotch from an inside pocket. Callan took a swig, then passed the bottle to me. I took a sip from the glass, depositing the fire water on my tongue and allowing it to sit there, so that the taste of it overpowered my senses.

'Westminster man,' I observed laconically after swallowing the blend, 'he speak with forked tongue!'

'The politicians have fucked us up the arse,' Callan seethed. 'If the public enquiry is critical of our activities, the boys across the water are going to leave us up shit creek without a paddle!'

'They're going to leave you up shit creek without a paddle,' I corrected. 'If the worst comes to the worst, I'll file a suit for compensation. Although I issue you with instructions, anyone who goes through the paper work will be left with the impression that I'm simply one of your patients. I set it up that way precisely so that I'd walk away with a golden handshake no matter how things panned out.'

'I want to kill you!' Braid hissed as he placed his hands on my throat.

I took a marionette from my pocket and made it dance about on the end of its strings. The doctor immediately let go of my throat, got up and did a little jig on the esplanade. Then I took a pin and jabbed viciously at the little wooden figure, causing Braid to howl with pain. I tossed the puppet into the Thames and James dived in after it. Fortunately, a couple of officers on a passing police boat were able to fish the patsy out before he had the chance to drown. Callan had guilt written all over him, a failed suicide attempt was not likely to impress the good men and women who would pass judgement on the doctor at the end of his trial.

Mitre Square is no longer what it was in the Victorian era, only one of its closed archways remains, while the modern offices and school yard that now dominate the local psychogeography are singularly lacking in atmosphere. Having led Sayyida Nafisah from Spitalfields Market to Bishopsgate, we headed south, only to find ourselves cutting back east along Bevis Marks. It was a very long time indeed since I'd been to Mitre Square and on that occasion I'd exited through Creechurch Lane, so it only seemed right that this time I reversed my previous route. I showed Sayyida the square, then led her along St James Passage to the Village

Bar, a pleasant café catering to a socially mixed clientele.

'Scrambled egg on two toast and a large cappuccino, twice.' We were eating in.

We sat by the window, our table was decorated with two large illustrations of fish. These were done in bright colours and had been given a cheerful cartoon-like treatment. This was in stark contrast to the murderous passions that fish bring to mind. I'm thinking of the smell that links finned and scaled creatures with the hussies who walk the streets at night. I set to work on my cappuccino as we waited for the scrambled eggs to arrive. I dipped into the whipped cream and chocolate at the top, spooning it into my mouth. Nafisah copied my every move, eating the top of the brew with her coffee spoon before proceeding to drink it once I'd lifted my mug to my lips.

'Could we have two more cappuccinos please,' I said to the waiter who brought our scrambled eggs.

I could feel myself getting an erection as I watched Sayyida tear into her egg on toast. I imagined the girl's body swelling out, with a huge belly and big pendulous breasts. My reverie was interrupted by the waiter calling me over to the counter to pay for the extra coffees, which were now ready. I ordered an ice cream for Nafisah, then made my way back to the table with the fresh cappuccinos. Later, as my companion sensually sucked the melting sweet from her spoon, I thought about rubbing the raspberry ripple between the girl's legs and then licking it out of her steamy twat.

'We've magick to perform in the square,' I informed Nafisah as she finished her pudding.

'We can't perform the sex ritual in broad daylight!' the girl protested.

'Don't worry,' I reassured her, 'we'll make ourselves invisible, so no one realises what we're doing.'

At first, Sayyida responded to the breath-taking simplicity of my plan with disbelief. It took a good five minutes to convince her that this particular ruse was a better piece of magick than the invisibility potions hawked by New Age quacks. A handful of office workers were enjoying the sunshine that was splashed across the square, but they quickly left when I unrolled a banner emblazoned with the slogan 'GO GO TRANSMISSIONS, PURVEYORS OF THE FINEST PERFORMANCE ART SINCE 1988'. Fortunately, Nafisah was already wearing a long and very wide skirt, so the bag of butcher's offal and sink plunger that I'd brought along as props were all we needed to carry off this scam.

I lay on my back with Sayyida, who'd thrown off her knickers, seated on my crotch. As I worked her love-hole, Nafisah pulled offal from the bag that had been placed under my coat and threw it around the square. As she saw fit, my companion used the sink plunger to assist in this process. As we made the beast with two backs, I was visualising Osiris and he physically materialised for a few seconds as I shot my load. Sayyida zipped me up and we'd both just stood up, when two policemen wandered into the square.

'What's going on here then?' the taller of the two demanded.

'Just a spot of performance art, officer,' I explained.

'Pull the other one, it's got brass knobs on,' the second cop cackled.

'Yeah,' his companion put in, 'don't try and bullshit us, we can see you're just some sicko, if you were a genuine performance artist you'd have had people videoing the event for posterity, not to mention someone doing still photographs. We get lots of Whacko Jackos around here and it would be tedious to arrest them all. I'll let it pass this time but I don't want to see you again. If you set foot inside the square when I'm on duty, you'll be nicked!'

'And by the way,' the shorter cop put in, 'it was Katherine Eddowes who had her entrails ripped out, not the other way around. Can't you perverts get anything straight in your minds?'

Clementia stood with her back to mine. I gazed across the room and reflected in a mirror I could see what Prudence saw. Like Freud, I believe in the female revenant, I believe that certain people are psychically drawn towards me and that our greatest happiness lies in the fact that every event that has ever occurred must reappear. Faith was with me now, just as four hundred years previously she'd been with John Dee. I was gazing back at myself in the mirror and I understood intuitively that Elizabeth and her astrologer had created an occult current between Richmond and Greenwich, using the sharp curves in the river on either side of London to set up a magickal system which enabled them to impose their Wills on the entire region.

As I gazed at the pleasant features reflected in the mirror, I felt a deadly and hostile current pass through me. I was conscious, completely conscious, I was in tune with a higher reality that told me some frightful peril was assailing Rachel Green. I did not know what it was, but I did know that it was something altogether awful, of which merely to think was to shudder. I wanted to go to her assistance, I tried to move, more than once; but I couldn't and I knew that I couldn't. I knew that I couldn't move as much as a finger to help her. Stop, let me finish, let me make the most of the present ritual. I told myself that it was absurd, but it wouldn't do; absurd or not, there was terror with me that night. I tried to ask Hermes to remove this burden from my brain, but my longings wouldn't shape themselves into words, and my tongue was palsied. I don't know how long I struggled, but, at last, I came to understand that for some cause, Hermes had chosen to leave me to fight the fight alone. I turned around, Eliza turned around, she saw the fear in my eyes. I told Beth to leave in the first rush of my fear, afraid, and I think, ashamed, to let her see my fear. She ignored my instructions.

I remember getting up from the sofa and following Rachel into the bedroom, and that's all I remember. I must have placed the plastic sheet across the bed earlier in the day, I have no recollection of doing this but it was a good idea, since it prevented the sheets from getting stained. I barely remember grabbing the knife and slashing at Rachel's throat and stomach before throwing the entrails across her shoulder. Then I took my tool box from under the kitchen sink and went back to the body in the bedroom. I figured that if I cut it up, it wouldn't be that difficult to dispose of the individual pieces.

Before setting to work, I went back to the kitchen and slipped on a pair of rubber gloves, I wasn't going to let my hands sink into the gunk that was still oozing out of Rachel's body without some form of protection. I wrapped some sheeting around the corpse and manoeuvred the body on to the floor. After spreading out several plastic sheets so that I wouldn't make a mess on the carpet, I began to hack into the girl's neck. Starting from the front, I got through to the spinal column without too much difficulty but by this time the blade on my hacksaw had gone blunt. I didn't have a spare blade and the one on the saw clearly wasn't going to go through any more bones. I threw down the implement and picked up an axe. Within a matter of seconds, I'd separated Holt's head from her shoulders. After that, I set to work dismembering the rest of the body.

Once I'd finished working on the arms, I sorted out the legs. Rachel was already naked, and I had an overwhelming urge to strip off my own clothes and roll around on the floor with her severed remains. I didn't have a condom, so I tore the thumb off one of my rubber gloves and slipped it over my dick. As I thrust my way into Rachel's bloody cunt,

I was riding on wave after wave of sexual pleasure. I wasn't just moving my pelvis up and down, I was hauling my whole body over Green's carved up bulk. I could have gone on all night, but instead of slowing things down for a few minutes, I just went with the flow of my desires, and shot my load into the thumb of that rubber glove.

I felt confused, so I got up and took a shower. As I washed the blood from my body, I began to put the events of the last few days into place. Just as the shamans of old learnt to climb the hidden tree that connected our world to that of the Gods, so I was learning the secret of consciously controlling the process of transition between my various per-sonalities. To the world at large I was Philip Sloane, a film-maker accused of murder who was on the run from the police. As I got into the shower, it was Philip's personality that controlled my body, but I was also Rachel Green the Witch. I didn't much like being Philip, I preferred being Rachel because only She had the strength of Will to make the most of every facet of my personality.

I hadn't been down to Amwell Street for some time. The last time I'd been to the pub it had been called The Fountain. It still had a lot of its original features but the clientele seemed to have changed. Rock and media types mixed with literary chancers, trendies enjoying the traditions of Old London. I just wanted to have a quiet drink but everyone there seemed to know me. I guess I must have a double called Roger who works in public relations. I sat on a stool at the bar and ordered a pint, by the time it was pulled, Vanessa Holt had slipped into the seat beside me and ordered a lager. I paid for both drinks.

'I was sitting in the corner, didn't you see me?' the girl demanded.

'I just came in for a quiet drink, I didn't know you were going to be here,' I blasted back.

'But we arranged to meet at eight, you're an hour late,' she protested.

'Stop giving me a hard time,' I crackled as the barmaid handed me my change.

'Don't you like me?' Vanessa queried as she ostentatiously placed her hand on my thigh.

'I don't wanna be your boyfriend, if that's what you mean!' I replied between swift swigs on my pint.

'I thought we were going out,' Holt lisped.

'Beats me where you got that idea,' I countered.

'So you want to split up,' she persisted.

'I'd want to split up if we were going out.'

'I want to split up too, which means we've got something in common.'

I downed the remains of my drink, got up and left the pub without saying a word. Vanessa followed me, grabbing my arm as I crossed the street. She tried to pull me against her, but I just kept striding southwards. I cut right down Margery Street, with Holt matching my pace despite my attempts to lose her. I found the New Merlin's Cave between Insurance and Fernsby Streets, but the tavern had closed down and the building looked like it was squatted. Looking up through the dusty windows there was some impressive silver decor in an upstairs room. Back at ground level, some loony had scrawled messages about London being the world centre of mind control.

'Bollocks,' I swore.

'What's up?' Vanessa enquired.

'They've closed down the New Merlin's Cave!'

'So what?'

'In the eighteenth century there was a famous spa here. There's also supposed to be a passage between the reservoir on Amwell Street and Merlin's Cave, an underground cavern beneath Penton Mount. This hill was sacred to the Druids.'

I showed Holt the building next to the pub, now derelict but once a thriving commercial enterprise, which for a price allowed the curious access to the English Grotto. Close to this spot one can find what are still quaintly described as the New River Water-works. I took Vanessa by the hand and led her through an extremely ambient housing block which must have been a hundred years old. The place was decrepit, and unlike Wilmington Square, which it abutted, it looked like a candidate for bulldozing rather than yuppification. Having traversed this picturesque ruin from north to south, we found ourselves on Merlin Street.

We stood on the site of the long-closed Merlin Street Baths, which had been one of a number of fashionable haunts for the upper classes in the eighteenth century. At that time the area had consisted chiefly of fields. Despite subsequently being built over, this psychogeographical hot spot still attracted those curious about rumours of an underground passage running beneath an ancient building. I leant back against a dirty brick wall, overcome by a powerful vortex of emotions. Vanessa knelt before me in that twilight of grime, undoing my flies and withdrawing my pork sword in one easy motion.

'In it the fountain has a thing,' I announced as Penelope swallowed my cock, 'which is most nobly contained. He who shall know it well, will love it above all other things. He who would seek and search it out, and being found put it afterwards into the earth and dry it to a most subtle powder, then again dissolve it in its water, but which has before been separated, then gather the parts together, which the earth shall set to rot in the water which should nourish it, is on the right path to knowledge.'

Penelope ran her tongue along my shaft. I heard a car door slam in Wilmington Square. I could feel Braid's breath, hot in the cool twilight of a May evening, rustle through my pubic hair. Behind us, a baby let out a series of cries. My prick glistened with Vanessa's spit.

'Thence there will a maiden breed,' I continued, 'bearing fruit at both her breasts. But that we should remove the rottenness, which neither she nor her fruit does care for, the maid I speak of in many things bestirs herself, and fervently desires it. For she mounts into the air flying on high; afterwards descending down gliding in the valley, and in descending down she fawns the fawn which Nature gives to her.'

I felt as if I was falling through cushioned air. I

imagined the coolness of the passage beneath me. The dampness of its walls. The waters of rivers flowing beneath London, long covered over but still making their way relentlessly towards the Thames. Vanessa took my manhood back into her mouth and swallowed it.

'It is a Dragon which has three throats,' I mewed, 'hungry and never satiated. All around him everyone assaults or kicks at him, surrounding him just as it were in a street and chasing him with a violent pursuit, so that a sweat do cover his face. Beforehand by heat one drives away the sweat which covers the face, which blackens and beglews it, as with bird lime then impregnates it.'

Vanessa shook my love muscle vigorously. Then she took the head of my tool and rubbed it against the roof of her mouth. I thought of Merlin, Maid Marion and King Arthur, and the legend of the sword and the Grail.

'In the same manner she brings forth again,' I moaned. 'This amorously done, much more powerful than before, then drinks it as the juice of the apple. So the infant according to its manner often drinks, and afterward brings forth again, so that it is clearer than crystal. And when it is so shining in a most strong and powerful water, it thinketh to devour its mother, who has eaten up its father and brother. So as it gives suck and broods, the Dragon strikes it with his tail. Into two parts divide its Mother, which does assist it after this division: deliver it then to the three throats, which they have sooner taken it than a gargle.'

'I want you to cum,' Penelope whispered as she took my meat from her mouth and worked it first with one hand, and then with the other.

I wanted to spunk up but I knew that the time for the final banishment had not yet come, and so instead of sperm, it was urine that boiled up through my groin. I watched in delight as the amber fluid splashed over Vanessa's face and hair, soaking her long golden locks with my pungent waters.

'And for that reason I would pray you, that you would be pleased to tell me, how they do call this Fountain, which is so amiable and wholesome.'

'Friend behold, since you desire to know it, 'tis most properly called the Fountain of the Lovers,' Penelope responded. 'How it must be known to you, that ever since our Mother Eve, that I have governed all the world, as great as 'tis in all the Circle, nothing without me can rule, unless God would inspire it. I who am called Nature O environed the Earth, without, within and in the middle. In everything I have taken my place, by the command of God the Father, I of all things am the Mother.'

Vanessa had closed her eyes but her mouth was still open, and as she spoke I directed the jet that streamed out of my prick into it, and a little went in, causing a momentary halt to the speech. Then I directed my flow back into Holt's hair, so that she was able to continue where she'd been forced to leave off.

'To all things I give virtue.' Penelope pronounced. 'Therefore nothing is or ever was without me, a thing which might beneath the Heavens be found, which is not governed by me. But since you reason understand, I will give you a goodly gift, by which if you will use it well, you may purchase Paradise, and great riches in this World. From whence nobility might rise, honour and great Lordships, and all pleasure in thy Life. For you shall use it with delight, and many noble feats behold by this fountain and the Cave, which governs all the seven metals.'

My force was spent, I could piss no more. Holt stood up and I kissed her brazenly on the mouth, then we headed back to The Fountain so that Vanessa might wash and dry herself a little, while I downed another pint. What had been used up, had to be replenished or the well of alchemical inspiration would run dry. The creation of gold must always begin with the transformation of a common and utterly despised substance. Urine had long been considered a potent medicine by lay healers, while sado-masochistic sex provided the means by which all these values could be transvalued. If science wanted to suppress alchemy without realising it, and New Age quacks wanted to realise alchemy without suppressing it, I alone understood that the simultaneous realisation and suppression of the alchemical process was necessary for its historic supercession.

# ❖ EIGHT ❖

I'D FORGOTTEN THE NAMES of most of the food stalls in Spitalfields Market, so I arranged to meet Sayyida early on Sunday morning in The Deli Dinner, a rendezvous which had the added advantage of being fully enclosed. I bought a cappuccino and an almond croissant at the counter, then sat down to consume this fare. Spitalfields Market on a Sunday is a middle-class oasis between the more proletarian Brick Lane and Petticoat Lane street markets. It's a covered market specialising in books, prints, organic vegetables and the like, the only place on the edge of the financial district to rival Greenwich, Portobello and Camden for weekend trendiness. As I downed my coffee, an old man sat down opposite me.

'God save you, stranger!' he said by way of greeting, and then proceeded with this discourse: 'If you have heard anything concerning the nuptials of the King, consider these words. By us the Bridegroom offers you a choice between four ways, all of which, if you do not sink down in the way, can bring you to his royal court. The first is short but dangerous, and one which will lead you into rocky places, through which it will scarcely be possible to pass. The second is longer, and takes you circuitously; it is plain and easy, if by the help of the Magnet you turn neither to left nor right. The third is that truly royal way which through various pleasures and pageants of our King, affords you a joyful journey; but this so far has scarcely been allotted to one in a thousand. By the fourth no man shall reach the palace, because it is a consuming way, practicable only for incorruptible bodies. Choose now which one you will of the three, and persevere constantly therein, for know whichever you will enter, that is the one destined for you by immutable Fate, nor can you go back in it save at great peril to life. These are the things which we would have you know. But, ho, beware, you know not with how much danger you commit yourself to this way, for if you know yourself to be obnoxious by the smallest fault to the laws of our King, I beseech you, while it is still possible, to return swiftly to your house by the way you came.'

'I long ago chose the second way,' I replied, 'and fear not friend, for although I read John Dee's mathematical treatise with great interest, my maze-like wanderings have always been on a straight course, for my methods are non-Euclidean.'

'God speed you on your journey sire,' the stranger said as he got up and left.

It was a sign from the nine masters that I was

indeed illuminated. I gazed after the stranger as he disappeared in the direction of the public toilets. A few minutes later, Sayyida emerged into my field of vision at the very spot where I'd last seen the old man. I bought two more cappuccinos and an almond croissant. As I was doing this, Nafisah greeted me and soon we were sitting on opposite sides of the table, gazing into each other's eyes. I could feel a slight tension in my body but this subsided when the girl bit into the snack I'd bought her.

'You look like you're enjoying that so much,' I beamed, 'that once we've finished our coffee, I want to take you across the market to the pasta stall so that you can fill your stomach with pesto and spaghetti!'

'Mmmm, sounds good,' the way Sayyida murmured the words nearly caused me to have an orgasm.

I had a vision of the girl eating spaghetti when drunk and as a consequence, splattering the sauce over her ample cleavage and stomach. I wanted to smother myself in cream and make Nafisah lick it all off. I was getting quite carried away with fantasies of force-feeding her chocolate cake, but the arrival of my assistants Sextus and Livy brought me back down to earth.

'Master,' Livy kowtowed, 'the membership of the Black Veil and White Light are becoming quite restless at your continued absence from the group's rituals. There is talk of revolt among the ranks, particularly from some of the wealthier members, many of whom are speaking about finding themselves a new master, one who pays more attention to their needs.'

'You know, Livy,' I announced as I fixed my disciple with a penetrating stare, 'that it is my custom to blame bad news upon the messenger. If you were any good, you'd have used my absence as an opportunity to take over the group. Since you have clearly failed to stage a coup, you are little better than dirt. Now go and prepare my magickal tools, I'll need them later.'

Having dismissed this flunky, I led Sayyida and Sextus to the pasta stall. Once Nafisah had eaten her fill of Italian food, I led our little party up Commercial Street and along Shoreditch High to the Slug and Lettuce. Once we were safely ensconced in my room, we all stripped off and covered ourselves in lard as preparation for astral travel into the fifties room of the Geffrye Museum, where we could engage in a spot of sex magick. We lay with our heads close together and our bodies radiating out into different parts of the room. My eyes were closed and it wasn't long before I found myself lying with Nafisah and Sextus on the rug in front of the fire in the museum's upstairs exhibition space.

Sayyida was sandwiched between me and my assistant. I lay on my side and manoeuvred her so that she was facing me. I grabbed Nafisah's huge tits and massaged them, her nipples were erect and I took first one, and then the other, into my mouth. I let my right hand slide down the girl's bulging belly and rubbed her clitoris. My hand came up between the girl's legs and I was delighted to discover she was all wet. I massaged some of the sex juice around Sayyida's clit, then slipped inside her. I humped for a few minutes, then withdrew, allowing Sextus to batter his way into Nafisah's arsehole, once he'd greased it with KY jelly.

After my assistant had taken the girl from behind, I forced my way back into her cunt. It took a while, but eventually we worked out a slow rhythm whereby I could move up as Sextus moved down, and vice versa. My assistant's balls were banging against mine and our pricks were separated by nothing more than a thin wall of flesh. It was very erotic and thus a highly charged act of magick. I was visualising the Goddess Isis, as were my two companions, and for a few fleeting moments she materialised above us as we fucked in the museum.

''Tis magick, magick that have ravished me!' Sayyida screamed as Sextus and I came simultaneously.

'Shut up, for God's sake shut up!' the guy in the room next to mine was banging on the wall as he hollered. 'I was out late last night and I want to sleep in, why can't you shag when you go to bed like normal people!'

I opened my eyes and simultaneously withdrew from Nafisah's cunt. Sextus wiped his cock with tissues before dressing. I dismissed my assistant, after assuring him that I'd attend the Black Veil and White Light ceremony that evening. Sayyida crawled into my bed. Once Sextus had gone, I got in beside her and we both fell asleep.

There were quite a number of things I required for the Order of the Black Veil and White Light ceremony we were holding that evening, so I went to Greenwich to sort this out. Having acquired candles and a variety of other ritual implements, I went into a newsagent's to buy a can of coke. It was while making this purchase that I realised I was being shadowed by the Syndicalist Youth League's portly intelligence department. I zoomed out of the shop and then stopped dead in my tracks. David White proceeded to career into my extended fist as he scuttled after me as fast as his bulky frame would carry him.

'You shit, you shit, you fucking shit!' White squawked.

'Watch where you're going,' I snapped.

'Listen Nolan,' White bellowed as sweat poured from his bulky frame, 'I know that you're the author of *Marx, Christ And Satan United In Struggle* because Callan is clearly just a minor corruption of your given name!'

'Did you know that believing Francis Bacon wrote the complete works of Shakespeare is a sure sign of mental illness?' I enquired.

'State asset!' White squeaked. 'You'll suffer for smearing me in this fashion, and what's more, I'm going to expose you in a pamphlet!'

'I'm terrified,' I assured the self-styled independent 'marxist' investigator.

'I bet you are,' as he spoke, White wagged his finger, a trick he'd no doubt picked up during the hours he worked as a school teacher, 'there's no power on earth that can resist the ability of rationalist enlightenment thinking to expose the truth!'

Since it's not possible to argue with loony conspiracy 'theorists', I made my excuses and left. White followed me, all the while screaming about the power of Diderot and Voltaire-style thinking to expose the 'Truth'. I went into a corner shop to buy some chocolate and while I was queuing up, the proprietor asked White to leave because he was upsetting other customers. Outside on the street, White had concealed himself in a pub doorway. I pretended not to notice him and made my way to the train station. I seated myself on a Charing Cross train and White attempted to conceal himself one carriage down from me. As the train moved away from the platform, I leapt off and waved at White as he pressed his nose against the window, a look of disbelief on his face as it dawned on the bozo that I'd out-smarted him.

Just as I was congratulating myself on evading a notorious loony, I ran into Vanessa Holt. I took the girl to the Noodle House, where I could get a kick from watching her eat and simultaneously insult the bitch. Holt left in tears, only to make her way up to my flat on Church Street. I bought some candles, then turned out of Church Street and into Brick Lane. It didn't take long to cut up past the bagel shop and down Redchurch Street to the Slug and Lettuce. Nafisah had woken up, I told her about the ceremony we'd be holding that night and she was very keen to participate in it.

I walked Sayyida down Redchurch Street and

along Nelson Road. Nafisah had Chicken Vindaloo with rice and garlic nan, I had a Vegetable Thali. We both had a sweet lassie. We finished with ice cream and coffee. It was a good meal but I was sexually satiated, and so for once I was able to watch my companion eat without getting an erection. Once I'd settled the bill, I led Sayyida along to Church Street – after cutting through the covered market, we made our way to the Naval College. Designed by Christopher Wren with the assistance of Nicholas Hawksmoor, this complex is the swankiest group of classical buildings to be found in Northern Europe.

The architectural ensemble is divided according to classical proportions by the five foot walk, part of a site line that runs through several of Hawksmoor's London churches. In fact, as I explained to Nafisah, the line bisects the British Isles, running from southeast to north-west. Its southern extremity marks the former site of Battle Abbey in Hastings, where Harold I died. From this historic location it extends through London and Glasgow to Uig, on the Isle of Lewis, where the oldest chess set in Europe was discovered. We ventured first into James Stuart's Georgian masterpiece, the rebuilt interior of the Chapel of St Peter and St Paul, dating from the first year of the French Revolution. Besides the sinister symbolism of the chiaroscuro paintings above the galleries and Benjamin West's *The Preservation Of St Paul After Shipwreck At Malta*, the chapel also contains a huge monument memorialising the disastrous expedition to locate the North-West Passage led by Sir John Franklin.

Having feasted our eyes on this occult laboratory, I guided Sayyida across to the mind control chamber known as The Painted Hall. The room was designed by Hawksmoor and its murals were executed by Sir James Thornhill, who was assisted in the upper hall by Dietrich Andre. Here one can find the whole gamut of occult symbolism, from classical pagan gods, via the signs of the zodiac and various royal personages, through to Galileo with his telescope. The utter contempt of the upper classes for the Christian religion they foisted upon the common man is plainly evident in this visual aid to alchemical processing. Every classical god from Zeus and Chronos through to Diana, Mars and Minerva, is depicted serving the interests of the burgeoning British state. After giving my companion a detailed account of the occult forces set to work in the room, I led her to Il Battello on the corner of Church and Creek Streets, where we indulged ourselves with cappuccinos and cakes.

We met where we always meet, at a secret location in the City of London. The venue isn't far from the Guildhall, so it won't surprise anyone if I reveal that it is close to Gresham Street. I'd made my way up from Cheapside where I'd been doing a spot of window shopping. Since it was the weekend, the streets were deserted and everything was locked up. The City of London has to be one of the safest places in the world, there are surveillance cameras everywhere, and the square mile has its own well funded police force.

'The nine masters await you,' James Braid said as he met me at the portal.

'That makes our total number ten,' I observed.

'Aye,' Braid shot back, 'Ten is made up of one and zero, the digits representing man and woman respectively. Add one and zero together and the sum comes to one, the figure of unity, the one that is All.'

'One does not turn one's back on the masters,' I railed as Braid hung back behind me. His presence was not required.

'I shall be waiting for you here at the turning,' Braid whispered as I made my way into the chamber that was forbidden to all but the Few.

I got down on to my knees and touched the floor with my forehead. A naked torch threw a dim flickering light around the cavernous chamber. I was told to rise and I did as I was told, for none dare resist the Will of the nine masters, who wait for the unwary at the Gates of Time. My spirit guides loomed before me in the gloom, their features shadowed by the cowls they'd draped over their heads.

'There are ten of us here,' the ninth master announced, 'and if a woman were to come into the room, there would still be ten, for while you a man are one, a woman is zero, nothing. The first principle of the world is nothing but if you have nothing, you must also have something, because nothing is a pure negation and a negation must be a negation of something. It is for this reason that Satan made Adam, the first man, out of Eve's spare rib. Now if you have both nothing and something, you must have a state of transition between them, and this state of transition is called becoming. It is from these three principles that the entire world is generated and it is by these means that we control your world of illusion.'

As the ninth master concluded his discourse, there was the single sounding of a gong, and a naked woman with long red hair burst into the room wielding a whip. The leather strip whistled through the air, tearing into my body. There was a second crack of the whip, a third and a fourth. My clothes were shredded in this onslaught and my body wracked with pain. I extended my arm to protect myself from an eighth crack of the whip and as a consequence, lost my sleeve. After the ninth crack, I was as naked as my opponent. On the tenth crack I raised my arm again and the whip coiled around it. I had a firm grip on the leather strip and gradually drew my adversary, who was determined not to let go of the other end, towards me.

I wrestled the vixen to the floor and once I was on top of her, she became completely submissive. I felt like taking her from behind but she begged to give me a blow job. I foolishly consented and once she had my prick in her mouth, she sunk her teeth viciously into the swollen flesh. I passed out cold. Later, I woke in a warm bed with earphones over my head, Dr Braid was employing the tried and tested technique of psychic driving. A three-minute tape loop had been playing constantly for the weeks

I'd lain unconscious, sustained only by a drip-fed feed.

The membership of the Order of the Black Veil and White Light can be divided very easily into two parts, an activist core and a broader periphery of the curious who contribute financially and as a consequence, stupidly believe that their money gives them access to our secret work, when in actual fact, they never see what it is that we are really doing. Membership of the Order is not cheap, and so every couple of months it is necessary to put on a show to amuse the profane who enjoy the trappings of occult initiation but are completely ignorant of its reality. That was what this particular evening was about, although I'd also invited a couple of journalists. The twenty guests were seated on folding chairs that encircled the stones placed at the centre of Pollard Street, wedged between Old Bethnal Green Road and Florida Street. It was an eerie spot with two huge health centres marking the boundaries to the north and south, while blocks of council flats fringed the east and west sides of this most barren public space. There can be no doubt that this is the omphalos of inner London, signalling as it does the essential emptiness at the heart of several former villages that have merged together to become a great metropolis.

'If there be somebody now,' I pontificated, 'which on the other side will complain of our lack of discretion, that we offer our treasure so freely, and without any difference to all men, and do not rather regard and respect more the godly, learned, wise, or princely persons, than the common people, those we do not contradict, seeing it is not a slight and easy matter. While we signify so much, our Arcana or secrets will in no ways be held common, or generally made known. Although the Satanic doctrine has been set forth in five thousand languages, and is manifested to everyone, yet we know very well that gross wits will not receive nor regard our message.

'Likewise,' I droned, 'the worthiness of those who shall be accepted into our Fraternity are not esteemed and known to us through other men's estimation, but by the Rule of our Revelation and Manifestation. Wherefore if the Godly and weak cry and call a thousand times, or if they shall offer and present themselves to us a thousand times, yet Satan hath commanded our ears, that they should hear none of them. Leviathan hath so compassed us about with his clouds, that unto us his servants no violence or force can be done or committed; wherefore we neither can be seen or known by anybody, except he that has the eyes of an eagle. It was necessary to set forth the Satanic Doctrine in everyone's mother tongue, because the unlearned should not be deprived of knowledge, when Satan has not excluded them from the power offered to the Dominant by this Fraternity. For this purpose, the illuminated shall be divided into certain degrees.

'When this is done,' I continued to rapturous applause from my audience, 'and comes to pass as that which is to proceed, thenceforth our Trumpet shall publicly sound with a great noise. When our secret Knowledge, which right now is shared by the few as a thing yet to come, shall be free and publicly proclaimed instead of being declared through obscure figures and pictures. What is as yet particular must be made general, and the Illuminoids who have secretly conspired against Christ's tyranny, will throw the Toad from his seat very shortly. Those gods who have hung from the Tree of Knowledge must be trodden underfoot. Their final fall has been delayed, and kept for our times, when they shall be scratched in pieces and renailed to the crosses from which they so wickedly flew. This is the means by which an end will be made of the Toad's cry, so that the many may hear our new voice in its full Glory!'

I waffled on in this fashion for the best part of an hour, then led my disciples through to a back room in the Fifth Man pub, which I'd decked out as a Temple. Here, we proceeded to invoke Leviathan. I pulled the hood of my cloak over my head and stood behind the altar, in reality a trestle table with a black cloth draped over it. There was a plastic replica of a human skull in the centre of the altar, and inverted crucifixes on either side. Once my disciples were kneeling before me, I raised my hands above my head and further theatricalities began.

'The condition of Nature,' I informed my congregation, 'that is to say, the condition of absolute Liberty, where there are neither Sovereigns, nor Subjects, is Anarchy and the condition of War.'

'Hail Leviathan!' my disciples chanted back at me.

'That Subjects owe to their Sovereigns simple Obedience in all things is the law of Satan, the Master.' I continued. 'And if Satan created the Earth and dwells everywhere within it, we are ourselves the physical manifestation of Satan.'

'Hail Leviathan!' the congregation howled.

'The profane who reject radical evil as the first cause and underlying principle of their nature,' I hissed, 'must cower as slaves before their master Leviathan, who we, as Satan embody through our control of the apparatus of the Democratic State.'

'Hail Leviathan!' the Initiates screamed.

'King of Hell!' I barked as I poured red wine into a silver chalice. 'This wine is the blood of the slaves. In the names of Lucifer, Astoroth, Baalbarith. Beelzebub and Elimi, we shall drink the blood of the slaves, who in rejecting the Laws of Nature, have reduced themselves to the status of mere fodder for our Passions.'

'Hail Leviathan!' my disciples whispered as I put the chalice to my lips.

One by one, the men and women who'd assembled to worship their own True Nature came forward and drank the wine. Having done so, they removed their cloaks, left the Temple and retired to the saloon bar to discuss the ceremony and other matters of magickal importance. I left Sextus and Livy to mingle with my deluded flock, who imagined themselves to be masters without slaves, when they were actually the slaves of my master. I took Sayyida Nafisah by the hand and led her into the night.

'The master is conscious of existing for himself,' I explained as we cut down Valance Road, 'however, this means much more than is implied by the coarse and utterly abstract notion of a life lived selfishly. Indeed, the master has independent consciousness precisely because his consciousness is mediated through another consciousness, that of the slave. To attain a state of illuminated mind requires recourse to the Other, and such encounters necessarily result in battles whose result must be the subordination of the slave to his master.'

'I see,' Sayyida replied in a tone which indicated that she was completely mystified by my revelation.

At the end of Valance Road, we cut across Whitechapel Road and headed down New Road. We turned right when we hit Commercial Road and headed for Berners Street. I was really getting into the stride of things, so I told Elizabeth that we were doing an occult ritual here because it was the site of Rudolf Rocker's legendary Anarchist Club, a centre for chaos, confusion and plots of mass destruction. Personally, I didn't give a toss about this long dead anarcho-syndicalist and I was quite consciously distorting the facts of Rocker's life as I described his activities and beliefs to Nafisah. It was better to do this than explain the true significance of the site, which was likely to frighten her.

Nafisah unzipped my flies, seconds later my cock was hardening in her hand. She looked at my erection, then looked me in the eye, and we both knew the answer to my question. I could feel the old urges welling up inside me, but I managed to resist them

as Sayyida worked my member in a steady rhythm.
Not yet, the time was not right, there were still some
things to be sorted out before Nafisah would be
called upon to become the ultimate sacrifice. I
looked at the girl and imagined her six months from
hence, with a swollen belly and huge breasts. I had
to feed her up before she could return from whence
she'd come. I could feel my back stiffening as
Sayyida increased the speed with which she worked
my meat. My seed splattered against concrete,
wasted but not wasted since the night was still
young. After we left Berners Street, I took Nafisah
to the nearest Halal fried chicken shop, where I
bought her a burger and chips. I watched with
delight as she licked the last greasy traces of this
meal from her lips, then told her I must go and that
she had to find her own way home.

I cut along to Osborn Street and walked briskly
up to Brick Lane. There were a couple of girls
standing forlornly against lamp-posts. The first
smiled at me as I approached her, she was wearing
a full length leather coat and her long blonde hair
was matted with dirt. I ignored her entreaties. The
next girl I saw was wearing a dress that was too
skimpy to protect her from the night chill. Her hair
was filthy and so were her faded clothes. I cut along
Church Street and used the pelican by the Ten Bells.
The darkness enclosing the locked gates to Spitalfields Market was suddenly banished as a middle-aged
whore lit a cigarette. She was incredibly ugly but
her jet black hair was clean and had been recently
cut. I was tempted, I have to admit I was tempted,

but I simply wandered down Brushfield Street to Bishopsgate and breathed in the financial success that was wafting out of the City.

I turned north and wandered up Norton Folgate to the Slug and Lettuce on Shoreditch High Street. Penelope Braid, a convincing double for Vanessa Holt, was standing outside the pub. She grabbed my arm, pulled me towards her and kissed me passionately, she used her tongue to prise apart my lips and then thrust it into my throat. She slipped her right hand into the front of my jeans and used the left to fondle my buttocks. Eventually she broke the embrace.

'Buy me a pint and a packet of fags,' Penelope demanded as she dragged me into the public bar.

'I'll buy you a pint if you promise to quit smoking,' I offered.

'You're mean,' Braid chided, 'what's the use of drinking if you can't enjoy a fag at the same time?'

I bought two pints of lager. There'd been a private function on at the pub earlier in the evening, and the vast amounts of left-over food were being offered around. I told Penelope I'd buy her twenty Silk Cut if she took on and beat the guy sitting at the bar who was challenging all and sundry to a sausage eating competition. The geezer in question, who was huge, seemed to find the notion of taking on a girl demeaning. However, the twenty pound note I brandished as prize money was sufficient to get the better of his scruples.

When I'd first met Penelope, you could see her cheek bones, but not any more. She'd filled out a great deal, in fact it was not unreasonable to call her plump, but she had to fill out a little more before I'd send her back from whence she'd come. As far as the sausage-swallowing competition went, Braid was at a distinct advantage in that she'd yet to finish her first pint and she hadn't eaten that day. In the five-minute time span that I'd allotted to the sport, Penelope wolfed down forty-six sausages against her opponent's pathetic twenty-eight. I bought my companion the fags she'd been craving, as well as a fresh pint. Then I handed her the twenty quid before disappearing into the bog for a swift wank. Seeing a woman literally putting on pounds as you watched was the horniest thing I could imagine, and I was determined to do something about my state of sexual excitement before Vanessa had the chance to take advantage of it.

'Buy me another pint,' Penelope demanded when I returned.

'Buy it yourself,' I retorted, 'I've just given you twenty quid!'

'You're mean,' Braid wailed, 'I need that money to pay off my debts. Go on, buy me another pint.'

''I'll buy you a drink if you'll have a gang bang with me and all the other geezers in the pub.'

'Sexist pig!' Penessa stormed as she stood up.

I took a ten pence piece from my pocket and flipped the coin so that it landed in front of the girl as she walked to the bar. However, Holt didn't bother to pick it up. She came back with a pint, informing me that if I wanted another drink, I could buy it myself. The landlord called last orders, so I got up and ordered two lagers. Vanessa was beaming as I came back with the drinks. She downed the pint she was holding in a long gulp. I put one of the lagers I'd just bought to my lips, and poured the other over Braid's head. As she gusted out of the pub, I offered to buy her a meal down Brick Lane. She ignored the suggestion, the banishing ritual had been successful. Soon, very soon, I'd be able to banish her for good.

# NINE

I KNEW VANESSA HAD A time-keeping problem, so I
arranged to meet her half an hour before the train
left for Cambridge. Unfortunately, she was thirty-
five minutes late. Holt wanted me to buy her a
drink, I insisted it was too early in the morning to
be boozing. We wandered out of the station and on
to Liverpool Street itself. Vanessa wanted to go in
the first café we came across, I insisted we cut
round the corner to Eldon Street. The east end of
this road is a little oasis of ordinary life in the heart
of the city. My companion suggested we go in
Appennino, then Brady's Bar, then Pret A Manger.
I dragged her past the Val Serchio sandwich shop
and into a store that had been imaginatively named
Ollie's Secondhand Bookshop.

I flicked through the literary novels, there were
some real turkeys, including stuff by the sub-
modernist suicide Richard Burns and the equally
talentless Bruce Chatwin. I'd already read Dennis
Cooper's *Closer*, but I considered it good enough to

be worth perusing again on the train. Vanessa insisted that I buy her a cookery book and a piece of feminist non-fiction, I forget the title. Having secured reading matter, we ducked into the Copper Grill. I just had a tea but I ordered an English breakfast for Holt. The caff is traditional, with checked wipe down tables. It was a pleasant experience indeed to watch Vanessa consuming egg, bacon, tomatoes and fried slice in an environment that belonged to some sixties time warp. I ordered a second tea and was overcome by a feeling of bonhomie.

'One day,' I said to Holt, 'I will take you to Gorhambury.'

'What's that?' a streak of egg yolk ran down the girl's chin as she asked the question.

'It's the Bacon family home,' I explained. 'It's just outside St Albans.'

'I'd like to go to St Albans,' Vanessa enthused. 'I hear there are more pubs per square mile than anywhere else in England.'

'We wouldn't have much time for drinking,' I explained patiently, 'the current Bacon family seat has a cubic room identical in its dimensions to the one in the Queen Ann House. It's obvious they were constructed as possible homes for the Arc Of The Covenant. Besides, there are lots of family portraits to be examined, not to mention old Shakespeare folios. In the grounds are the ruins of the old family home, the one Sir Francis actually lived in!'

'It sounds a bit boring!' Holt pouted.

I wasn't going to let the girl's ignorance spoil my mood. I had a feeling our Cambridge caper would be great fun. The train ride out of the London suburbs and up to the Fens was as tedious as ever, but I had the Dennis Cooper book to amuse me. Having arrived in Cambridge, we walked briskly to the gates of Trinity College. A crowd of forty students had gathered beside the famous Cambridge apple tree, grown using the seed of an apple from the tree whose fruit inspired Newton to propound his theory of gravity. There was a great deal of restlessness within the crowd, since I'd spread a rumour among the undergraduates that something very strange indeed was going to happen on our ascent of the state's favoured site for ritual human sacrifice.

One red-haired young man appeared particularly perplexed as we set off on foot. The men who fell in at the front and rear of the procession looked out of place, they were too old to be students. Nevertheless, they obviously knew where we were going. Two of them led the way up to Cambridge Mount, a pre-historic earth structure that clearly represents the womb of Mother Earth immediately prior to the fruitful gathering of the harvest. Once we reached the peak, with its breath-taking view of Cambridge and the surrounding countryside, the four older men stood outside the circle formed by the students.

'As I have already demonstrated,' I announced, 'Sir Francis Bacon mapped out the intellectual tasks of the generations who were to succeed him. However, since the role of the universities is to restrict the flow of knowledge, it comes as little surprise that Bacon is more or less ignored by the contemporary philosophical mafia.'

As I spoke, one of the four older men pointed at the red-haired student, who immediately bolted down the Mount towards the car park at its base. Three men raced after him, while the fourth pulled a mobile phone from his pocket and used the speed dialling function to alert colleagues sitting in a Ford estate that their quarry was heading down the hill. The student was caught by the men who leapt out of the car, and bundled into the back seat. The estate sped off, and was followed shortly afterwards by a second car that the men who'd come up the Mount leapt inside. Their Escort skidded as it made a fast ninety-degree turn on to the road.

'The work of the alchemist Sir Isaac Newton,' I continued, 'is shrouded in obscurity. While the Cambridge professors allow students to study Newton's output on natural philosophy, his alchemical texts such as *The Book Of Daniel* and *The Great Pyramid*, are treated with complete disdain. Then there is the case of Aleister Crowley, banned by the Dean of Trinity from the college grounds . . .'

Unfortunately the incident involving the red-haired young man had rather distracted the attention of my audience. Instead of wasting my breath, I distributed some Order of the Black Veil and White Light literature among the students, along with lodge application forms, knowing full well that only those undergraduates with rich parents would have the means of meeting my membership fee. I left Vanessa Holt to carouse with the students and made my way back to London.

I got back to Greenfields and found Dr James Braid, or rather Braid's double, in my flat. The doppelgänger knew that I was a victim of mind control and would react obediently if he ordered me about in a suitably authoritarian manner. Anyone, like me, with a high Hypnotic Induction Profile has a suggestible personality, and it is individuals of this type who tend to be picked out by the security services for brainwashing. For the sake of convenience, I will refer to this double by my dead controller's name. Braid told me to remove my clothes, when I'd done so, he examined me closely. I had a birth mark on my back that Braid claimed wasn't recorded in Philip Sloane's detailed personal records.

'Lie down on the bed,' Braid instructed and once I'd obeyed the order he continued by telling me, 'relax, you are feeling tired, you are feeling very very tired. Your eyelids are heavy and you want to go to sleep. Relax, relax every muscle in your body. Relax your feet and feel the relaxation moving up your legs and into your body. Breath rhythmically. Relax, relax your stomach and chest. There is a warm sun beating down upon you. Relax your neck and feel the relaxation spreading to the tip of your head. Now that you are in a deep sleep, I want you to tell me all about yourself.'

'It is in vain, Vulcan,' I burgeoned, 'to pitch your

net in the sight of the fowl thus. I am no sleepy Mars to be catched in your subtle toils. I know what your aims are, sir, to tear the wings from my head and heels, and lute me up in a glass with my own seals, while you might wrest the caduceus out of my hand to the adultery and spoil of Nature, and make your accesses by it to her dishonour more easy. Sir, would you believe it should come to that height of impudence in mankind that such a nest of fire-worms should with their heats called *balnei cineris*, or horse dung, profess to outwork the sun in virtue and contend to the great act of generation, nay, almost creation? It is so, though. For in yonder vessels which you see in their laboratory they have enclosed materials to produce men, beyond the deeds of Deucalion or Prometheus, of which one, they say, had the philosopher's stone and threw it over his shoulder, the other the fire, and lost it. And what men are they, think you? Not common or ordinary creatures, but of rarity and excellence, such as the times wanted and the age had a special need of, such as there was a necessity they should be artificial, for nature could never have thought or dreamt of their composition . . .'

It was obvious to Braid that the agency I was being run by had programmed this crap into me, knowing full well that I'd be placed in a hypnotic trance by anyone wanting to recover information about my mission in the world of occult cranks and psychopathic petty criminals. Braid tried to take me back to my childhood, so that he could talk me through to the present, but this path through my theatre of memory had been thoroughly blocked. It would have taken months, if not years, to unravel my programming and Braid simply didn't have that kind of time. Instead, he thought he might as well see what messages my masters had stuffed me with.

'Say whatever it is you've been sent to tell me.' Braid impacted.

'There has to be a sacrifice,' I announced in a self-confident voice, 'and for there to be a sacrifice, there must be a Sacred Executioner. I am the sacrifice and you are the executioner. Man is inherently violent and ritual killing is simply a means of curbing this violence. I am to be sacrificed for the good of the community, as a means of resolving conflict, and you must carry out the execution. You will become a scape-goat for undertaking a taboo deed that leads to a greater good and you will be banished from this community. Nevertheless, you will be protected, and so no harm will come to you.'

I got off the train at Kings Cross. I wanted to obtain an alchemical novel called *White Chappell, Scarlet Tracings* by Iain Sinclair, so I walked along to the bookshop on Caledonian Road. Sayyida Nafisah was at the counter buying another book by the same author, *Lud Heat and Suicide Bridge*. It was an attractively packaged paperback. I asked my former disciple if I might look at it and she turned her back on me, then bolted into the rear of the shop, where a lot of anarchist magazines that no one in their right mind would want to read are stocked. I followed Nafisah up the step.

'Piss off,' she duked, 'I'm not in the least bit interested in you. All this stalking you're doing is just an attempt at psychological intimidation.'

'Leave the young lady alone,' the shop assistant, an ageing Stalinist called Fred, throbbed at me.

'Look,' I said, placing myself in front of the counter, 'you've got no business interfering in my private affairs. Sayyida used to be my girlfriend, we split up after I discovered she was a state asset who'd been planted on me to monitor the effects of the brainwashing I'd undergone at the hands of the notorious Dr James Braid.'

'I'm not interested,' Fred yawned.

'I'm being persecuted by the state,' I tried to keep my voice flat as I made this dramatic revelation. 'My mail is being intercepted, I've been abducted by the police and placed in an isolation ward where I'm being programmed with a new personality. Sayyida is part of the plot to destroy me so that the Conservative party can win the next general election.'

'Have you thought of buying a soap-box and taking it down to Speakers' Corner?' The shop assistant addressed me in the most mocking of tones.

Fred was pretending he didn't believe me. Obviously, he was playing a key role in a carefully orchestrated plan to drive me mad. The shop assistant was a state asset. I wasn't going to waste my breath on him, so I went and stood outside the door, waiting for Nafisah to come out. I would make the girl confess the truth to me about her role in a sinister plot cooked up by the security services. It was down to me to make the world safe for democracy.

I clearly heard the shop assistant warn Sayyida that I was standing outside the door waiting for her. All of a sudden, she seemed interested in books, something that I'd never noticed before. She flitted from one tome to another, examining each carefully. I cut across the street and concealed myself in a pub doorway. Twenty minutes after I had apparently departed, Nafisah felt it was safe to come out of the shop.

'Stop, stop!' I shouted after the girl as she speeded off down the street, her gait bearing an uncanny resemblance to that of a demented duck.

It would have been a hard task catching up with Sayyida had I not guessed that she was heading for the tube station. I took a short cut down Donia Street only to find that my prey had disappeared into thin air, so obviously all those occult works she'd been reading had done her some good. I trudged back to the bookshop, where I found Fred making his way out of the door for his lunch break.

'Look,' I whispered at him, 'I have something very important to tell you about your friends in the secret state, they've mastered the secret of invisibility. I just ran down a little used route to cut Sayyida off at the station and she completely eluded me.'

'I'm not surprised,' Fred hee-hawed, 'since she told me she was getting a bus to Islington, so she turned left and not right when she got to the end of Caledonian Road.'

'That's the kind of lie that proves you're a state asset!' I cried triumphantly.

I followed the shop assistant into a pub where he was greeted by a number of pimps, prostitutes and other unsavoury low-life characters. I decided discretion was the better part of valour and beat a hasty retreat, so that I might live to fight another day.

Penelope Braid was hungry, so I took her to the Astro Star Café on the Bethnal Green Road, very close to the local branch of Tescos. My companion complained that there was no cloth on the table, so I explained that the establishment catered to a working-class clientele who didn't care for such fripperies. I just had a cup of tea, but I ordered mushroom omelette, chips and peas for Braid. I get a sexual kick out of watching girls eat. Seeing a nice middle-class girl forking cheap working-class nosh into her mouth, appealed to the pervert in me. I was also fascinated by the old men eating around us, all of whom had very distinctive characters.

'You ever been to Canary Wharf?' a pensioner sitting across from us shouted to another old man. 'I went there, it's a very funny place. There's lots of strange noises, you hear a lot of canaries tweeting.'

'I go to Madeira for my holidays,' you could have cut the thick cockney accent with a knife.

'What are you talking about now?' the man must have spent most of his life in London, but his soft brogue was a dead give away that his childhood had been spent on the other side of the Irish Sea.

'Madeira is in the Canary Isles,' the cockney shot back, 'there are a lot of tweeting birds there.'

I shot my load as Penelope mopped up a blob of tomato sauce with her last chip, then I watched her eat ice cream. Young girls might be cute but personally I have always preferred the larger bodies of mature women. While intelligence and the personality are ungendered, at least until they become deformed due to the baneful effects of patriarchy, there are obvious biological differences between a man and a woman. Young girls look pretty much like boys, it is only when their bellies and breasts swell that I feel compelled to unite in sexual union with my other.

'Why did my father want me to meet you?' Penelope asked as she finished her ice cream.

'We're old friends,' I explained as I touched her gently on the arm, 'and since you'll be going up to university in a few weeks, he wants me to show you the difference between a man and a woman.'

'But I already have my degree,' Braid protested.

'You have one degree,' I admitted, 'and you are about to start your postgraduate studies. However, the true initiate has 360 degrees. There is far more to occult initiation than the 33 degrees of Free-masonry!'

'Pray, tell me more,' Penelope sussurated.

'Beneath the crossroads in Royston,' I explained, 'lies a Templar cave which was later transformed into a Rosicrucian cavern before being filled with earth to hide the secrets of the hieroglyphs carved into the chalk surface. The bell-shaped cave was excavated by the Templars as a site for ritual human sacrifice. In the dead of night, your father and some friends plan to break into the locked cavern. There I will make love to you beneath the watchful eyes of all present. I will fuck you from every position known to man, but most importantly from behind, because this is the most potent form of sex magick. We will shag for hours and you will be groaning with pleasure, then finally your father will step forward and despatch you to the spirit world, where you will become an incredibly powerful entity. All of this, of course, you must do willingly.'

'I don't wanna die,' Braid informed me.

'You must die,' I chided, 'if you are to be reborn. You will become a Goddess, ruling the lives of earthly men and women. As you become increasingly powerful, I will impose your Will in this our earthly realm.'

'Let me think about it,' Penelope pouted.


I met Vanessa as she came in off the train from Cambridge. We cut across Bishopsgate and through the back streets to Spitalfields. On the corner of Church Street, a group of American tourists were listening to a guide tell them about the horrible murders that had taken place in the area. People were coming in and out of the Jack The Ripper pub with cups of tea and coffee. I've always found the bar in that establishment somewhat bleak, on the black walls there are old newspaper clippings but apart from a few seats against the wall, the floor space is empty, which makes it all the better for packing in tourists.

'In the eighteenth century,' the murder guide announced as he pointed down Church Street, 'these houses were built for rich silk merchants. In 1888 they were slums. Twenty years ago you could buy one of these houses for fourteen thousand pounds, today the same house will cost you three hundred thousand pounds. That gives you some indication of the changing fortunes of this area.'

Christ Church was locked up and under repair. It looked like it had been neglected for years. At the other end of the street, a huge crowd of Muslims were emerging from the Jamme Masjid Mosque, previously the Great Synagogue and actually built in 1743 as the French New Church for Huguenots. This was an area where for hundreds of years the process of cultural hybridity had led to fantastic innovations in the life-styles of the polyglot crowds who gave these streets their vibrancy. There was a resonant quality to the place that you couldn't find in any other part of London.

'How did it go with the students?' I asked Vanessa as we headed for the East End Kebabish, probably the best value Indian in Brick Lane.

'Fine,' Holt assured me, 'I visited some student digs where I had a gang bang with seven or so boys. They definitely like me. I'm sure several of them will cough up the membership fee for initiation into our order. Most of them seemed more interested in orgies than magick, promising them pussy heaven seems the best way to part them from a huge chunk of their parents' cash.'

'The profane are all sleeping men,' I observed laconically.

I ordered two specials, vegetable curry, and some nan bread. We ate in silence, since I knew most of the things I had to say would offend the devout Muslims who ran the cut-price restaurant. My succubus had really swelled out since we'd first met, I was almost ready to banish her to the spirit world. I decided that on the morrow, I would take Vanessa to Walberswick, so that I might get rid of her forever.

From Brick Lane we cut back down Church Street and on to Greenwich High Road. Pistachios Café opposite the Treasure Of China restaurant was closed. I'd yet to check out the Bar du Musée. In the end, I led Holt across to the Coach and Horses pub in the covered market where I called heartily for pints of ale.

'The beer drinker,' I announced after standing on a conveniently placed table with my pint in my hand, 'is mounted and *ale*-vated to such an *ale*-titude that he will talk of religion beyond belief, interpret the Scriptures beyond all sense and show you points of law above all reason that can be *ale*-edged!'

We drank rowdy toasts to tapsters, bezlors, carousers and wine-bibbers, bench-whistlers, lick-wimbles, down right drunkards, petty drunkards, bacchus boys, roaring boys, bacchanalians, tavern ancients, captains' swaggers, fox-catchers, pot and half-pot men, quart, pint and half-pint men, short-winded glass men, privy drunkards, half-pot companions and other good fellows of our fraternity. After several rounds, I led a huge company of newly acquired friends along to the Admiral Hardy on College Approach.

I'd just been handed a pint when I got a call from Dr Braid on my mobile. I made my way to the hospital, where Braid was waiting for me. I followed the doctor down a corridor and into an empty ward where he told me to sit down on a bed. I don't remember what the doctor said, we exchanged a few words and then I was led into another ward by Sister George.

I was given a sedative and fell asleep almost instantly. In my dreams, Sister George came by and put an oxygen mask over my mouth. When I woke up, I pulled the oxygen mask from my face and tried to speak. Sister George took my hand, or maybe she was taking my pulse. A passing nurse tried to put the oxygen mask back on but Sister George told her to leave me alone.

Sister George motioned to a doctor, who exchanged a few words with her and then led me out of the ward to a group therapy session organised by a Scottish psychologist who used very experimental methods. The treatment began with all the patients sitting in a circle and discussing what they wanted to do. Several were of the opinion that the people we had murdered should be brought back to life through the use of highly advanced medical techniques. Other patients objected to this idea because the subjects of the proposed experiments had already suffered irreparable brain damage and would never lead a normal life. A particularly disturbed man claimed that none of us had really killed friends or family members, but that others had been put to death in their stead.

We talked for twenty minutes until we were interrupted by an old soldier who came into the ward and saluted us. The corporal checked to see if everything was ready, and the process of collective decision-making completed. The NCO could find no fault with our conduct, so he gathered up the mugs from which we'd been swigging tea and put them into a case. Soon after this, orderlies brought ladders, ropes, and poles into the ward, which they laid down before us.

'Right, you 'orrible little men,' the corporal announced, 'each of you must carry one of these three things with you for the rest of the day. You are free either to make a choice of one of them, or to cast lots about it.'

'We'll make our own choice,' we replied.

'No,' the corporal instructed, 'let it be decided by lot.'

Then he made three little schedules. On one he wrote 'Ladder', on the second 'Rope', on the third 'Pole'. These he put in a hat, and each man had to draw one, and whatever he got, that was to be his burden. Those who got the ropes imagined themselves to have the best of it, but I chanced to get a ladder, which afflicted me greatly, for it was six feet long, and pretty weighty, and I was forced to carry it, whereas the others could lazily coil their ropes about them. Then we were led out into the hospital grounds and set to square bashing. It wasn't long before those with the ropes cursed their bad luck, for it was they who were most likely to suffer blows from the ladders and poles.

After about half an hour of this night drill, a nurse had me pulled out from among the ranks and I was told to lay my ladder down. She took me into the hospital and left me sitting alone in a sparsely furnished room. Sister George appeared about ten minutes later with a pot of tea and some biscuits. She didn't stay long. Once she'd gone, I poured myself a cuppa and dunked a biscuit into the brew. Then the nurse who'd brought me up to the room returned, she gave me a paper chit and several plastic bags filled with my possessions. Sometime later, a different nurse came in with some forms and instruction booklets. I took these and put them in my briefcase.

I poured another cup of tea and drank it. I stared out of the window and although it was still light, I can't remember anything about the view. The first nurse came back and asked if I wanted to say goodbye to Sister George and Dr Braid. After I'd said that I did, she led me back down to the ward where we made our fond farewells. I was ready to go back out into the world with a minimum amount of support from my controllers. They wanted to be certain that no one would trace my murderous activities back to them. I was put into a taxi that took me to Shoreditch, a journey which late at night took less than twenty minutes.

Soon after I got in, my door bell rang. I pulled a couple of beers from the fridge and went down to the street. I pulled the door firmly shut behind me to prevent Sayyida from pushing her way into the flat. I took Nafisah's hand and led her along Redchurch Street. She started to speak when we stopped to negotiate the traffic on Bethnal Green Road. I put a finger to my lips and Vanessa fell silent. The traffic was really thundering along this road, but things were much quieter on Brick Lane.

We were confronted by the crowds of late-night revellers and cabbies making use of the twenty-four-hour bagel bakery, but once we'd negotiated this throng, the street was silent since the flock of Indian restaurants had closed for the night. We walked earnestly past the front entrance to the disused brewery. Gainsborough's portrait of Sir Benjamin Truman now hangs in The Tate Gallery instead of Brick Lane, poetic justice since there was once a monastery on the brewery site. We cut right down Hanway Street. My old haunt, number twenty-nine had been demolished. I led Nafisah to the brewery gates, a side entrance, immediately in front of where that haunted house had once stood.

We sat down on the pavement and I put my arm around Sayyida's shoulder. I opened the bottles of beer and handed one to Nafisah. She sipped at the brew and then began fiddling with the long, thin and very loose skirt that was wrapped around her legs. I took a swig of beer and gazed across the street. Everything was still and silent. I looked down at Sayyida's lap, she'd arranged her skirt so that it fell on either side of her legs, she wasn't wearing any knickers, so I could see her quim in the moonlight. I looked up and Sayyida pressed her mouth against mine. As we kissed, I twisted around and found myself on top of Nafisah, this was a perfect piece of sympathetic magick, exactly what I'd planned. Split-seconds later, my jeans were around my ankles and Sayyida had my cock in her hand, which she guided into her dripping wet cunt.

Nafisah fell back so that she was lying with her back on the ground and her legs splayed out. My bare knees scraped against the pavement as I worked my cock in and out of Sayyida's hole. I did my best to roll up and down Nafisah's body, to give her a bit of clitoral stimulation, rather than just pumping up and down, but it wasn't easy since doing so caused me to graze my legs. I guess I was doing alright, since Sayyida's moans shattered the silence of the night. We fucked like this for ten or fifteen minutes, I deliberately held back rather than going with the immediate flow of my desire. I didn't want to cum inside Nafisah's cunt, so I pulled out and stood up. Sayyida sat up and took my tool in her mouth, as she sucked I could feel my whole body tense and then relax as I shot my load.

I grabbed my bottle of beer, straightened up with my trousers still around my ankles, and took a swig of lager. I lent back against the gate that towered above us and my cock glistened in the moonlight. I was pleased with myself, I could feel something in my subconscious attempting to turn me into Philip, but I'd learnt to overcome this programming.

# ✣ TEN ✣

I MET VANESSA HOLT at Liverpool Street, having given her strict instructions not to be late or she would never see me again. I ignored the familiar sight of the back streets of Bethnal Green and Stratford as the train pulled out of the station, my attention being absorbed by a novel entitled *Deliria* by Albyn Leah Hall. Vanessa sat across from me unable to decide whether she wanted to read a cookery book or *F/32: The Second Coming*, a piece of experimental fiction by someone calling herself Eurudice. The train was bound for Norwich and it was rather full. Outside the window, if I'd bothered to look, I'd have seen typical London sprawl. The first stop was Colchester, after the train pulled out of the station, we entered an alien landscape resembling something dimly remembered from childhood. Suffolk, in all its charm, appears typically English if you make the mistake of taking the paintings of Constable as being representative of the country.

I felt like a time traveller as I led Vanessa out of

the train at Ipswich. We'd entered another world, one bypassed by the twentieth century, where witches and hobgoblins still haunted the night and the tensions of village life were resolved by unseen and only seemingly random acts of violence. Vanessa wanted to get a taxi into the centre of town but there weren't any outside the station and I couldn't be bothered to wait for a bus, so we strode over the Orwell and wandered past the football ground. Since I hadn't visited this city before, I didn't know where I was going but I kept to a straight path, since this was the way destiny led me. When I say straight, I mean this subjectively, since the town retains its Anglo-Saxon lay-out and it isn't possible to stride forward with the same certainty as one might feel on a Roman road. As we made our way through winding passageways, I kept weaving from side to side, so that these perambulations might approximate a straight line.

Before long we found ourselves at Christchurch Mansion, now a museum. The building is filled up with a great deal of eighteenth and nineteenth-century rubbish, works by Gainsborough and even worse local artists such as Cedric Morris and John Moore, not to mention piles of old household junk, crockery, furniture and other knick-knacks that went out of fashion years ago. I led Vanessa through what until a little over a hundred years ago had been the Fonnereau family seat. This Huguenot family had fled to escape the persecution of Protestants in France. Having established themselves in England as merchants, they'd bought the building with its acres of ground from the Withypoll/Devereux lineage in 1735. However, what interested me had never been a feature of the house. The Hawstead Panels had been removed from Hawstead Place near Bury St Edmunds in the early seventeenth century and were subsequently purchased by Ipswich Museum during the 1924 Hardwich House sale. These alchemical paintings were made by Lady Drury early in the seventeenth century, a member of the notorious Bacon family, her uncle Nathaniel Bacon was the court painter. Lady Drury pursued her occult interests while her husband was away on state business. Her only child Elizabeth was consumed during the course of this frenzied search for the philosopher's stone, and John Donne was commissioned to produce an elegy for the dead girl.

'What's so interesting about these pictures?' Vanessa demanded.

'They are alchemical paintings,' I explained.

'It says here that they're emblematic panels,' Holt contradicted.

'Idiot,' I cried as I cuffed the girl round the head, 'do you think the true significance of such works would be advertised to the general public? Why, they've even re-ordered the sequence of the images to make it harder for the profane to penetrate to the inner heart of these mysteries.'

Having seen these glories, everything around me paled into insignificance. There was no point hanging about the mansion, so I led Vanessa to St Mary le Tower Church in the town centre. This had been sacred ground since at least the thirteenth-century, but little of the original church remained. It should go without saying that a member of the Bacon family paid for it to be rebuilt in the Victorian era. The church had originally been topped by a spire, and I felt it necessary to impress upon Vanessa the symbolic significance of its transmogrified form.

'In the tarot,' I testified, 'there is a card that bears the picture of a tower with its battlements struck by lightning. Two men, one crowned, the other uncrowned, are falling with the fragments of broken masonry. The attitude of the former imitates the shape of the letter Ayin. This card contains the first allusion to a material building in the pack. It signifies the invisible or spiritual whorl. The sixteenth card represents the fall of Adam. He will become increasingly corporeal until the eighteenth arcanum, in which he attains the maximum materialisation.'

'You treat me like an imbecile,' Vanessa shrieked. 'Why can't you explain in plain English what on earth it is that you mean. I'm very intelligent, I don't understand why you treat me like I'm thick.'

'The irresistible current touches all those who expose themselves to its vortex on the terrestrial heights,' I put in good naturedly. 'If you are impure, you are threatened with disorganisation more or less complete, according to your intellectual or moral unworthiness. If on the contrary, you are worthy of the higher regions, the baptism of fire renders you one of the Magi, the sources of terrestrial life are at your disposal, you become a Therapeut.'

'Am I ready for the test?' Vanessa sounded unsure of herself.

'I have told without any error,' I was hood-winking my companion, 'how the body shall get a soul, and how you must separate them, and divide them from one another. But the division without doubt, is the key of all our work. It is performed by the Fire, without it our art would be imperfect. Some say that Fire produces nothing but ashes. These charlatans are wrong, for Nature is engrafted in the Fire. If Nature were not there, the Fire would have no heat. I will take Salt to bear me witness.'

I led Holt down to the Wet Dock, built in 1842 and often cited by vulgar materialists as the key to the prosperity of the town in the second half of the nineteenth century. Although the Wet Dock has long been used as a port, it was actually constructed to expedite the mass drowning of women who after dying, were ravished by the demons of the under-world. To repay the people who indulged them with these ritual sacrifices, the sex-starved Furies saw to it that there was abundant wealth for the upper class males of Ipswich.

'Let's eat,' Vanessa commanded as she attempted to drag me into Il Punto, a brasserie on board the M. S. Amuda which is permanently docked on the quay.

'Good idea,' I agreed 'but not here'. I'd taken in the special offer of a three-course meal for £13.95 and it didn't appeal.

'What about this place,' Holt suggested pointing at the land-locked Mortimer's restaurant.

'We'll go to the Neptune Café,' I announced mag-nanimously, 'it's only round the corner.'

'When was the last time you came to Ipswich,' Vanessa brayed as I led her on to Fore Street.

'I've never been to Ipswich before,' I insisted.

'In that case,' Holt retorted, 'how on earth do you know your way around.'

'Beats me,' I replied, 'perhaps I came here in another life or maybe I've studied a tourist guide.'

As I watched my companion eat eggs, beans and chips, I marvelled at the weight she'd put on. She was no longer the asexual girl I'd first met, she had the seductive figure of a mature woman. I was ready to banish her from this world for good. Some moron had left a copy of the *Ipswich Historic Churches Trail* on our table and Vanessa glanced at it as I finished my coffee.

'Let's find St Stephen's and hit the trail outlined in this guide,' Holt suggested.

'Are you mad?' I retorted, 'the whole thing smacks of alchemical processing, they get you to visit sacred sites in the city just as the pilgrims of old did. What you see is imprinted on your mind in a very specific order and you'll never be capable of independent thought again!'

'It only takes half a day to complete the trail,' the girl protested.

'We haven't time,' I snorted, 'there are more important places for us to visit.'

Before we went to pick up our hire car, I couldn't resist giving Vanessa a foretaste of what was to come on a far grander scale, so I took her from the café up Orwell Place, Thacket Street, Dogs Head Street, St Stephens Lane, Dial Lane and along Tavern

Street to The Walk and The Thoroughfare. These mock Tudor ensembles were built in the nineteen-thirties and fail to convince because unlike the genuine article, the walls don't sag and their wooden beams are too cleanly cut. From a distance they might just about fool the untrained eye, but close up there is something very sinister about these fake Tudor buildings.

Clencairn Stuart Ogilvie had inherited the Thorpeness estate in 1909 and immediately conceived the plan of building upon its grounds a mock Tudor Village for middle-class holiday-makers. Just up from the historic town of Aldeburgh, the complex is centred upon the Meare, an artificial lake constructed around the story of Peter Pan. Another notable feature of the Thorpeness holiday complex is the House In The Clouds, a former water tower capped by a house. To the east of the village is the sea, and the River Hundred flows by it.

Our first port of call was The Gallery Coffee Shop, one of two cafés in the village. The ground coffee was passable and I certainly needed a pick-me-up after the drive from Ipswich. Next we walked down The Whinlands to The Almshouses – the view was impressive but everything was spoilt when we passed through the gate and found ourselves on a council estate. I wasn't prepared for the dull normality that lay beyond the alien landscape of mock Tudor facades. While I appreciate the necessity of housing proletarians close to any middle-class refuge, since they are needed to clean and maintain the place, this was a little too close for comfort. One was left wondering if it was the child of a street cleaner who was responsible for the fire that had burnt out the Dolphin Inn and Restaurant, the only pub in the village. It is telling that the Workman's Club opposite this ruined shell had been left untouched by the vandals who'd wrecked what had long been the centre of mock village life.

We made our way up an unmade road known as Westgate. At the top of this is the towered Westbar, a military style medieval gatehouse tower designed by William Gilmour Wilson in 1929 and now a Grade II listed building. We cut through this to the Country Club, the scene of a famous suicide by a soldier who shot himself rather than face the Hun during World War II. Zig-zagging somewhat, we made our way up the hill to St Mary's Church, one of the ugliest ecclesiastical buildings I'd ever seen. This non-denominational nonentity had been erected in 1939, designed in Neo-Norman style and partially constructed from concrete, it is a monstrosity. Somehow it had become a listed building but this hadn't prevented vandals from attempting to burn it down. The door was open and the church felt extremely cold inside.

'This place is utterly useless for sex magick,' I informed Vanessa, 'it has no atmosphere whatsoever.'

'It's ugly as sin,' Holt concurred.

Next, we made our way to the Meare Shop and Tea-room where we enjoyed cuppas and homemade cakes before heading for Dunwich. Rather than the mock horror of historical nostalgia, we faced the all too real terrors of storm and flood. Dunwich had once been a prosperous city, indeed King Sigebert had made it his capital after ascending to the throne of East Anglia in 630 AD. Little is known about the settlement after it was taken by the Danes, but by the eleventh century it was bustling, with many wealthy merchants living within its walls, while its harbour was filled with the ships of numerous nations. But storms ravaged the town, first in 1328, then 1357 and 1560. Disaster struck again in 1570 but the greatest inundation was that of 1740, when most of the city was lost to the sea. The coastline is still eroding at the rate of one metre a year.

This psychogeographical dislocation sent me into a reverie. I remembered a past life when as a sailor I'd been working on a boat that formed part of the Dunwich Icelandic fleet until disaster befell it. I walked Vanessa along the shingle beach at Dunwich, recent rains had brought about further erosion of the cliff face. Human bones were clearly visible where a fresh swathe of a graveyard had been washed away. We stood on the ruins of a house that had been exposed by the action of the sea. I searched in vain for odd portions of the round Templar Church claimed by the sea in the mid-seventeenth century. Although parts of the stonework have been recovered in recent years, what remained was now under the water and there was no chance of making the beast with two backs on its former site.

I wanted a pint of Adnams, so we made our way from the beach to the Ship Inn. The local brew is sweeter than most bitters, but after the initial shock you get to like it. The Ship with its nautical paintings and fixtures, including a port hole between the bar and the restaurant, is quite fun but I desired a more exotic location, so we trundled into the car. First we found a restaurant in a nearby village. It was a little crowded but the service was good and the food excellent.

'A real Balti!' Vanessa exclaimed as she tucked into her chicken curry. 'A proper Balti is served in the dish it was cooked in, it's a joke when you go into an Indian restaurant only to find the dish your hot Balti has been served in is cold!'

'Look,' I said as I used a spoon to make an excavation into my Korma, 'this is the real test that the food has been cooked in the dish, the coloration around the edge should be different at the top and the bottom. This one passes.'

'You're right,' Holt confirmed, 'and mine passes with flying colours too.'

'Tastes good!' I yelped as I tore a strip from my nan and dipped it into the Korma.

I could feel myself getting an erection as Vanessa slopped a piece of nan around her dish, then shoved the princely delicate into her O-shaped open mouth. I took in the way Holt's breasts and stomach had swollen up since I'd placed her on a regime of forced feeding. I loved her huge arse, the love handles spilling over the top of her Levi jeans, her massive thighs and arms. The girl had put on several stone since we'd first met.

'Penny for your thoughts?' Vanessa whispered.

'Don't worry about me,' I mumbled, 'just eat, eat!'

'I feel stuffed!' Holt confessed as she patted her pot belly.

'But you're so skinny!' I screeched. 'You must eat everything up and then I'll buy you a pudding.'

Once we'd gutted ourselves with ice cream and coffee, we made our way to The Fox in Darsham. This is a theme pub that was done up in the seventies to make it look like it was old. There are roof tiles on the top of the bar and foreign currency stuck to the walls. I ordered two pints of Adnams. After draining mine, I ordered two more and went for a piss. The toilet is quite charming, there is even a towel rail with a towel on it. The place is very homely. I returned to my drink and began working myself up to what I'd do later that night. The hour was approaching and I wanted to make sure I was well lubricated for the festivities to come.

Last orders were called and we got another pint before making our way to the car. Vanessa's final destination was Walberswick, now a small village but once a great town. I drove casually to St Andrew's Church, there was no hurry, I had all the time in the world. The first Walberswick Church had been built at the end of the marshes, right next to the sea. This eleventh century church was dismantled four hundred years later because it seemed likely it would fall victim to Neptune. Three churches have been constructed in Walberswick since the first, all on the same inland site, the last now stands surrounded by the ruins of its larger predecessor, and it was on this spot that I had resolved to banish Holt.

It was midnight and my naked companion's corpulent body reflected the moonlight delightfully. We approached each other where an altar had once stood. As Vanessa caressed me, I reflected that William Wykham had become Vicar Of Walberswick in 1382, the very year in which his name-sake and double was active in Winchester. My lips met those of the doppelgänger and I drew my right hand up between her plump legs. Her sex was wet and as I removed my hand I could see it was red with menstrual blood. Holt pulled me down and we rolled on the grass.

'But to the false hypocrites,' I announced as Vanessa suckled on my bloody finger, 'and to those that seek other things than wisdom, we cannot be made known but their wicked counsels shall light upon themselves, and our treasures shall remain untouched and unstirred, until the Lion doth come.'

I was forced to cease my speech as Holt kissed me passionately and forced her tongue into my mouth. I was almost smothered as her fleshy form enfolded me. Next, I felt her tongue on my chest, then my stomach and I could not help but think of where her mouth was headed. She caressed the top of my pubic thatch, finally licking my length. Before long, she had the tip of my cock in her mouth whilst she worked the base with her hand.

'For us this is the whole sum and content of our rule,' I announced, 'that every letter and character which is in the world ought to be learned and regarded well; so those are like unto us, and are very near allied unto us, who do make the Satanic Bible a rule of their life, and an aim and end of all their studies, let it be a compendium and content of the whole world. And not only to have it continually in the mouth, but to know how to apply and direct the true understanding of it to all times and ages of the world.'

Vanessa was bent over me, her head bobbing up and down the length of my throbbing manhood. I grabbed the girl's thick legs and pulled her around. At first Holt resisted, but it wasn't long before her cunt was pressed against my mouth, her menstrual blood running over my lips and spilling down my chin. Soon, very soon, I would anoint her with my milk. The girl raised her head, just as I'd hoped she would, while continuing to work my tool with her hand. I sucked her swollen clit into my mouth and she groaned with pleasure. I imagined Vanessa's face with my cock pointed directly at it like a gun. I would anoint that face, that gateway to the soul, which is universally taken as the physical embodiment of the whole personality.

I felt the force of an orgasm welling through me, the tension rose in my groin and white dirt, life contaminated with the ambiguity of death, exploded out of my urinary tract and spurted into Vanessa's well-fed face. One minute I could feel the full weight of her ample body pressing down against me and the next, the succubus was gone. At last, after long struggle, the She-Demon was banished! I fell asleep on the damp grass and was still groggy as strong hands pulled me to my feet.

'Jesus,' a cop exclaimed, 'not only is he bollock naked, he's got blood all over his face!'

I knew I was in a tricky situation, there was no point explaining that I'd just banished a She-Creature from the 'other' side. My story was simply that I'd been hitch-hiking and the woman who'd picked me up had pulled a gun, made me strip and then forced me to lick her out in the churchyard, which no man in his right mind would have done because it was her 'time of the month'. Finally, she'd drugged me, which explained why I was asleep when I was found. I don't think the PC who arrested me was convinced by this narrative. However, I used my statutory phone call to alert Sayyida Nafisah to my plight. Her family were able to pull the necessary strings to secure my release.

I was driven back to London and it was three-thirty in the morning when I was released into Sayyida's custody. There was one thing that had to be sorted before I could collapse into bed. Mary Ann led me through the streets of Whitechapel to Bucks Row. We kissed and it wasn't long before Nichols had her hand on my flies. I could feel myself trembling as she took my cock out and examined it in the moonlight. Then my companion hitched up her skirt and I thrust my manhood into the black depths of her cunt. Afterwards, I made my way back to my flat on Brick Lane, while Nafisah disappeared into the blackness of night.

I woke up in a strange bed. There wasn't anyone beside me. I got up and drew the curtains. Dawn was breaking and I was looking out over row upon row of terraces. There wasn't much in the bedroom except for a weird selection of clothes and some alchemical prints on the wall. In the main room there were various magickal implements and a lot of books. I scanned the spines, works by Eliphas Levi, Papus and Julius Evola were among those on display. The titles of their books made it plain that these authors wrote on esoteric matters, as did the fact that the handful of names that meant anything to me all belonged to famous occultists. Among the later were Aleister Crowley, H. P. Blavatsky and Dion Fortune. I closed my eyes, reached out and pulled a book from a shelf. This turned out to be *The Secret Of The West* by Dmitri Merezhkovsky, which at that time appeared completely incomprehensible to my untutored eyes.

I went through a filing cabinet, the top three drawers were filled with documents detailing the history and rituals of a group that was registered for legal purposes as the South London Antiquarian Society, although it operated under a variety of other names including the Lodge of the Black Veil and White Light. A name that cropped up on many of these papers was familiar to me but this failed to prepare me for the shock I was to experience upon opening the bottom drawer. The individual in question shared more than just my name, he'd co-opted my identity. I stared down at a copy of my own birth certificate, a document I'd only been able to obtain upon reaching maturity at the age of eighteen. There in an old fashioned script was a name I'd never divulged to anyone – Geoffrey Reginald Thompson.

I threw down the sheaf of papers I held in my hand and walked across to the telephone, picked it up and dialled my own number. While the exchange system clicked through the digits I'd punched out on the push button phone, I picked up a set of keys that were lying next to an address book. I played with them idly as I listened to my own voice on the answer-phone. I could feel anger surging through me as a beep indicated that there was room on the tape to leave a message.

'You're gonna die you fucking besuited experimental film-making shitbag. I might have been born in London like you but I still honour the ways of our Druid forefathers in Ireland, while you've completely lost touch with our roots. I'm gonna kill you with a hostile and deadly current of Will!'

Then I went back to bed. I hadn't had much sleep and I needed all I could get. I set the alarm, knowing I'd feel worse than I did now upon waking up in two hours time.

# ❖ ELEVEN ❖

I'D SLEPT THROUGH MY alarm and it was Sayyida who woke me. She'd let herself into the flat with the key I'd given her the night before. Nafisah threw clothes at me and called a cab. It didn't take long to speed through the city, across the river and along to Waterloo. We only just caught the train. I needed the coffee and cheese roll that Sayyida brought me from the buffet. I felt terrible but knew that everything was working out just as we'd planned. Nafisah put on her veil before getting off the train, which was just as well since a hireling had been sent to meet us at Winchester station.

This city had once been the capital of England but was now a sleepy town known chiefly for its public school founded by William of Wykeham in 1382. The local cathedral is the final resting-place of William Rufus, son of William the Conqueror, who was shot in the New Forest by Walter Tyrell and as every Initiate knows, this was not an 'accident' but a carefully orchestrated act of ritual king slaughter.

Today, those who continued this tradition would suffer a severe shock when they discovered that I'd substituted their divine surrogate with someone else. The hireling drove us to the foot of St Catherine's Hill, from where we followed the public footpath to the maze cut into the turf at its peak. Around the unicursal labyrinth thirty men dressed in sheets had gathered. They imagined themselves to be bards of the Gorsedd but looked more like members of the Ku Klux Klan. Various greetings were made and I was given my own set of sheets to don. Once I'd robed myself in the bed clothes, there was a loud bang on a gong and the throng around me fell silent.

'Sacrifice in the Christian utopias is conducted after the following manner,' the chief Druid announced, 'Hoh asks the people which one among them wishes to give herself as a sacrifice to God for the sake of her fellows. She is then placed upon the fourth table, with ceremonies and the offering up of prayers. The table is hung up in a wonderful manner by means of four ropes passing through four cords attached to firm pulley-blocks in the small dome of the temple. This done they cry to the God of mercy, that he may accept the offering, not of a beast as among the heathen, but of a human being. Then Hoh orders the ropes to be drawn and the sacrifice is pulled up above to the centre of the small dome, and there it dedicates itself with the most fervent supplications. Food is given to it through a window by the priests, who live around the dome, but it is allowed a very little to eat, until it has atoned for the sins of the State. There with prayer and fasting she cries to the God of heaven that He might accept its willing offering. And after twenty or thirty days, the anger of God being appeased, the sacrifice becomes a priestess, or sometimes, though rarely, returns below by means of the outer way for the priestess. Ever after, this woman is treated with great benevolence and much honour, for the reason that she offered herself unto death for the sake of the Pan-Celtic cause. But God does not require death.'

'No,' the chorus shot back, 'God does not require death but we do, our Mother the Earth must be fertilised with the blood of one of her daughters!'

'Aye,' the arch Druid boomed, 'for we do not worship the God of the Latins! While the Celtic Church has been an effective front for many hundreds of years, we remain true to the religion of our fathers! Blood will out and blood must bleed, so that the Celtic nations may be reborn!'

Blood, blood, blood!' the chorus howled.

Then the assembled Druids sang a hymn to Love, another to Wisdom, and one each to all the other virtues, and this they did under the direction of the ruler of each virtue. Next each took one of the women who emerged from the trees behind them, and they danced for exercise with propriety and stateliness under the blazing blue sky. The women wore their long hair all twisted together and collected into one knot on the crown of the head, but in rolling it they left one curl. Once they threw back their hoods, it could be seen that the men had one curl only and the rest of their hair was shaven off.

'The sun is the father,' the chief Druid announced

once the dancing stopped and the gong was sounded a second time, 'and the earth the mother. The air is an impure part of the heavens, all fire is derived from the sun. The sea is the sweat of earth, or the fluid of earth combusted, and fused within its bowels, but is the bond of union between air and earth, as the blood is of the spirit and flesh of animals. The world is a great animal, and we live within it as worms live within us. We hold as beyond question the immortality of souls, and that these associate with good angels after death, or with bad angels, according as they have likened themselves in this life to either. For all things seek their like. Evil and sin come of the propensity to nothingness, sin having deficiency as its cause. Deficiency of power, wisdom, or Will. He who knows and has the power to do good is bound also to have Will and therefore cannot sin.'

Sayyida Nafisah was led to the centre of the maze and ordered to strip. There were cries of puzzlement as she was led naked through the labyrinth to the gallows at its end. The crowd was expecting to see Penelope Braid, whose father was keen to have his only daughter transformed into a powerful entity in the spirit world. During the confusion I managed to slip into the trees, where I abandoned my suit of sheets before speeding down the hill.

'That's Sayyida Nafisah,' someone cried. 'We can't sacrifice this girl, her father hasn't consented to it and he's a very powerful man!'

'You're right,' the chief Druid roared, 'the whole ceremony is ruined since there isn't enough time to prepare a substitute, the astrological conjunction takes place in six minutes!'

I scrambled through scrub land and over fences. I knew the Druids would have my guts for garters if they caught me. I reached the main road and stuck my thumb out. A few cars passed but I was lucky, the fifth pulled up and I got a lift as far as Wimbledon. I only had to change once on the tube to get to Turnham Green. Penelope Braid was waiting for me at my flat. I gave her a detailed account of her father's involvement in the old religion. It had been at great personal risk that I'd gone to Walberswick to banish the demon who possessed my beloved, but everything had turned out for the best and the girl I'd saved from the fires of hell accepted my offer of marriage.

I closed my eyes and relaxed, when I opened them again Penelope had disappeared but a man I recognised as Dr James Braid was sitting opposite me. He was my controller, the man from whom it felt as if I'd spent a lifetime trying to escape. I followed Braid to his car and he drove me to his office in Belgravia.

'You look tired,' Braid said sympathetically, 'you need a vitamin shot.'

'I don't want to kill her,' I sobbed as I was strapped to the operating table, 'I really don't want to stab her.'

'You don't have any choice,' the doctor told me as he swabbed my arm, 'you thought you'd broken our cycle of control but we've programmed every episode of this sorry saga.'

'I don't understand.'

'This is the next stage of our mind control experiment,' the surgeon explained, 'we want to teach our patients to consciously activate different personalities we've programmed into them, so that they can make the most of any situation they encounter during the course of their espionage activities.'

'It's not a natural part of my make-up to commit murder!' I wailed.

'Nonsense,' Braid snapped, 'have you no grasp of the mechanism of mimetic desire?'

'No,' I replied.

'We value objects,' the doctor explained, 'because other people desire them. We learn this system of value by imitating other people, we don't so much desire objects as desire to be like other people. But wanting what other people want leads to conflict. To bring conflict to an end there has to be a surrogate, a sacrificial victim, a final killing to bring order into society. You've been programmed with a personality that is identical to the one we've implanted in the mind of my daughter. This will necessarily lead to conflict between you and Penelope, a conflict that you can only resolve through her immolation!'

'It's horrible,' I moaned, 'it's too horrible!'

'No it's not,' Braid insisted, 'it's an act that will justify all the funds that have been poured into my research! No matter how hard you try to resist, in the end you will do my bidding!'

'No I won't!' I protested as I felt a needle being slipped into my vein, and after that I can remember